I0586058

The Beauty Of Tears

(The Italian Family Series)

Lucy Appadoo

Copyright © 2016 by Lucy Appadoo. All Rights Reserved.

No part of this publication may be reproduced, distributed, or transmitted in any form or by any means, including photocopying, recording, or other electronic or mechanical methods, or by any information storage and retrieval system without the prior written permission of the publisher, except in the case of very brief quotations embodied in critical reviews and certain other noncommercial uses permitted by copyright law.

This book is dedicated to my father, Antonio, who inspired the events in this story that is a work of fiction. I am blessed to have him in my life, and grateful to him for sharing his wisdom and love.

Contents

Chapter 1

NEW BEGINNING - 1948

R oberto was on his way home to meet his father by way of a donkey. He patted the donkey's ear and rode down the sloping path to his house. Frost covered the cobblestones on the uneven ground. He was not far now, but was already sighing at the earliness of the hour.

As the donkey plodded through the streets, Roberto noticed everything in his little village. He noticed the grey, cracked ground and the stone wall beside cream-coloured flat-topped houses. The houses had long, narrow double windows and balconies. In the distance were tree-topped mountains, and sloping paths that made lazy hikers stumble. The village of Eboli was serene in Roberto's eyes, a place of absolute peace, even at its most crowded. The

ferny tree smell signified a fresh new morning, and the
beauty of nature.

He took a deep breath as he reached home, then tied the
donkey to the nearby post and hurried up to the rough
stone house he shared with his family. It was a small house,
with only two small bedrooms for the five of them. With
so little money, they were barely able to buy food and the
basic necessities.

He shivered as he opened the weathered wooden door
and stepped into the cold, dense air of the living room.
His family was gathered in the scantily furnished room,
his father standing by the fireplace, his mother and his
sister Angela with heads bowed down over needlepoint.
His older brother, Filippo, was writing on a notepad, while
his younger brother Edoardo lounged on a sturdy wooden
bench which was covered with a crocheted blanket. With
its worn concrete floors and thin walls, the house held little
heat. Roberto could almost see the warmth leaking out
around the window and door frames.

His father turned towards him. "What took you so long,
Roberto? We must hurry for the wood."

Edoardo moved his lanky frame and pushed himself off
the bench. The top of his head came only to Roberto's
chest, but the finger he jabbed at Roberto's midsection
said he wasn't daunted by his smaller size. Even though he

was only ten years old, he tried to act older. He shook his head, green eyes darkening. "Why do you get to go with dad, and we don't?"

His father drew a hand through his auburn hair. "Because you are younger than your brother, and I only need one of you. You keep going to school."

Filippo hesitated, then walked up to his father. "But, Papa, I am older than Roberto. I'm sixteen, and old enough. Can't I help?"

While Roberto waited for his father to respond, he glanced toward his mother and sister. They looked so different. Angela, at nine years old tugged at her long, jet-black curls, and his mother's face was half-hidden by long copper hair highlighted with gold. Their anxious expressions were the same.

Papa glanced at Filippo, a pained expression on his face. "You, Filippo, must keep going to school. Roberto has always liked working with his hands."

His mother looked up at her husband. "But Roberto should have a chance to go to school. He's only thirteen."

Papa cleared his throat, avoiding her eyes. "Maria, we discussed this."

She put her hands up in protest. "But we didn't really discuss it, did we? Can't we find other ways to make the money? Hire someone else."

His father sighed. "And then pay them an adult wage. It's not possible. Not possible."

His mother stalked towards the door to the hallway, then turned back. "You need to take more risks in business. How else do other businesses prosper? You don't take any risks Giovanni, so how can you expect success? Fear doesn't make you move forward."

She walked off, sighing. Roberto looked back at his father's distant gaze and sagging posture. "It's okay, Papa. I don't mind helping. I do like school, but I want to help the family as well. Let us go then."

Roberto didn't like it when his parents fought, and that was often nowadays. They always seemed to disagree on the business, but his Papa was doing the best he could. Roberto didn't mind helping out the family, but he did miss his friends at school. Still, if he helped out in the business, his parents might not fight as much. They'd finally have more money to buy nice things and Mama wouldn't complain about not having warm clothes or enough food.

His father led him outdoors, and loaded pieces of wood into a box, then attached the box onto the donkey's back. Papa tugged the donkey forward. It balked for a moment, pulling back against the rope, then lowered its head and plodded along beside Papa. Roberto tagged along behind.

Together they started towards the village. "Papa, why can't I make this trip on my own?"

Papa sighed again. "Roberto, you must listen and listen carefully." Roberto waited as he took in the mountainous views, enjoying the chill winter breeze, soft against his cheek. "You are now working with me, and because this is your first day, I must make sure you deliver the wood to the right people."

"If only I could go to school and help you as well."

Papa looked straight ahead. "I'm sorry, but for now this is how it must be."

Roberto nodded. "I still don't understand why Filippo couldn't help you. He's older. All my other friends are still going to school."

His father swallowed and avoided his eyes. "It just is the way it is, Roberto."

Roberto pushed him further. "Help me understand, Papa. What is really going on with the business? For many years, you didn't need my help so why now?"

His father cleared his throat. "Roberto, please leave it alone. Now let's get on with it."

"But Papa—if I'm old enough to work with you, then I'm old enough to know what's going on."

For a long moment, only the donkey's hoof beats broke the silence. Then Papa said, "I can't do it on my own.

We need the money, and with two of us working, we can double our funds. Do you understand that?"

"But you were doing much better before. What changed?"

"You don't give up do you?" Papa shook his head and looked away. "Someone is hurting the business. I think people are getting most of their wood from someone else."

"Do you know who it is?"

Papa shook his head and fell silent.

Giovanni's face felt warm. He wished he could answer his son. Who would do such a nasty thing to someone who had a family to take care of? It was bad enough having to ask his son for help. Now Roberto had to hear about someone sabotaging their business as well? It wasn't something a twelve-year old should have to worry about. His eyes burned with shame.

Giovanni knew Roberto wanted to go to school like his friends. It wasn't fair but Giovanni had no choice. He couldn't afford to pay someone else. Edoardo was too young, and Filippo needed to stay in school. His gift for mathematics needed to be nurtured.

No, Giovanni knew he had made the right choice. Roberto was good with his hands and had a good head on his shoulders. He enjoyed spending his time outdoors, savouring the natural scenery. Despite Roberto's disappointment, Giovanni knew the boy was proud to be able to help out his family. The sacrifice would only be temporary; Giovanni told himself. Just until he got back on his feet.

Roberto gave the donkey a scratch. "What do they need the wood for, Papa?"

Giovanni suppressed a smile. His son never ran out of questions. "Well, the businesses need the wood for their ovens to cook bread. It's their living, just like selling the wood is our living."

"And we will make good money if others don't sell wood?"

Giovanni stopped and stared at his son, pensive. "Reasonably well. Not rich, but we will survive, my son. We will survive."

Roberto had another thought "Papa. I'm happy to help, but you spend money on the wood, so how is that helping us?"

His father smiled. "I buy the wood from the lumberjacks, but then I sell it for more than I spend on it. Then we can make a small profit."

Roberto nodded and continued to walk alongside his father, who laid a gentle hand on his shoulder. He noticed his papa's sad expression, and had often wondered why his father didn't smile very much. He wondered what more he could do to help the family survive.

When they reached the village, his father called on a customer, who stood beside his steps, wearing a worn, grey cap, and waiting for them to unload his delivery. Papa unloaded the donkey and handed the customer the box of wood. The gentleman handed Papa the money, and Roberto saw the colour drain from his father's skin.

"This is not what we agreed upon," Papa said.

"Well that's all you're getting. Take it or leave it."

"But we agreed to five lire, not three."

The gentleman sighed and shook his head. "I don't have five, so either take it or have your wood back. I can always get it from someone else."

His father didn't say anything for a moment, and lowered his head "Fine, sir. I will take the three lire."

"Very well." The man left abruptly without saying goodbye.

Giovanni looked stricken, and Roberto didn't know what to say. He wished he could've spoken to the man. Maybe he could've changed his mind so his father could be paid what was owed.

After a few more sales around the city, his father and Roberto stopped for lunch outside the house of Italo, Papa's friend who had brought them food. Italo rushed off on an errand while Roberto and his father enjoyed the outdoor scenery. They savoured some ciabatta bread with sun dried tomato and buffalo cheese. Roberto topped his bread with cheese, a sprinkle of pepper, basil, and several pieces of the sun-dried tomato before devouring it. He didn't usually get to enjoy such a treat. The tomatoes were tangy and salty on his tongue. If only they could afford to buy some.

They ate in silence for a while until Roberto broke the quiet.

"Papa, why didn't you fight for five lire back there? You shouldn't have given up. Why did you?"

His father took a long time to answer. "Sometimes, my son, you need to learn to make peace. Appreciate what you're given and not what you can get."

"But Papa, it's not fair. You probably didn't make a profit on that sale."

His father sighed and put down his bread. He looked over into the distance before staring straight into his son's eyes. "Roberto, promise me something."

"Yes, Papa."

"Promise me that you will take care of your Mama."

A niggle of worry fluttered in Roberto's stomach. "What do you mean?"

His father avoided Roberto's eyes. "Just promise me."

"But why? You take care of her now."

His father scratched his stubbled chin. "If anything ever happens to me, I want you to take care of your Mama. Maybe you will be stronger than me with the sales, but I am a humble man, and I simply take what I can get. Do you understand that?"

Roberto's heart beat fast. "I think so, Papa."

"Good. Now, there'll be no more talk about the profit or business. We must do what we can, and keep the peace for the sake of the community. People talk, and if people talk, then that can affect our business."

"Okay, but—"

"But nothing." His father rose from the table. "Come, we must get back to work."

Roberto wiped his mouth with the back of his hand and rose too.

At the end of the day they led the donkey back from the village. They didn't talk much, but Roberto didn't mind the quiet. They'd said everything there was to say, and now he could focus on the natural views of the towering trees, hilly terrain and silent surroundings. Before he could think any further, he and his father were interrupted by someone he recognised in the distance. Roberto's best friend, Andrea.

Andrea strolled towards them, favouring the leg he'd broken several years ago, and patted Roberto on the back.

"Roberto, my man. How are you doing?"

"Andrea, what are you doing here? Shouldn't you be in school?"

"Ah—the school isn't the same without you. Come back, man." Andrea had the bluest eyes Roberto had ever seen. His hair was black and shiny, and he towered over Roberto. He was a good athlete too, except for the slight limp he had.

"I wish I could." He looked at his father who gave Andrea a welcoming smile.

"Good to see you Andrea. How's your father doing?" Andrea's eyes darkened. He turned away, avoiding Roberto's eyes. "He's fine sir. He says hello, and would like to buy some branches from you."

"Oh."

"Yes, he'd like to use them for something, but I can't remember what."

"Okay, you tell him I shall be over soon for a special visit."

Andrea nodded and fell into step beside them.

When they reached Roberto's house, his brothers and sister were sitting on the sturdy wooden bench making a telephone out of tin cans with a long piece of string. Roberto ignored them and headed towards his room with Andrea. They sat side by side on the bed. As Andrea shifted his weight, the sleeve of his shirt lifted slightly to reveal a sharp bruise on his right wrist. Roberto gasped.

"What happened to your wrist Andrea?"

Andrea grunted. "Oh, this old thing. It's nothing. Just fell over, that's all."

Roberto chose his words carefully. "You would tell me if anything was wrong, wouldn't you?" Silence. "Andrea?"

Andrea's laugh sounded forced. "Of course I would. Come on, why don't we play some bocce before you have your dinner?"

"There's not enough room. We'll have to go outside."

"Let's go then."

As they were about to leave, Roberto heard his parents' raised voices from the next room. His mother had just arrived home from an errand, and she seemed to be arguing with his father. Their words were muffled by the wall, but Roberto could slightly make out what they were saying. He stopped Andrea from leaving and they stood near the door, both listening.

His mother said, "We cannot keep living like this. Do you want us to starve?" There was no response from his father. "Why can't you be a stronger man? Fight for your family?"

"But cara, I am doing my best. Why can't you appreciate that?"

"Well your best is not good enough for now, Giovanni."

Tears stung Roberto's eyes. He closed them, and leaned his forehead against the door, his muscles tense. He didn't even care that Andrea was there, witness to his grief.

Roberto felt Andrea's hand on his shoulder but he ignored it. He wasn't feeling sociable. His dad was doing his best and what was his mother doing? Berating him, and showing no appreciation for all his hard work. So what if his father wasn't rich? He was the best man—and the best father—Roberto knew.

Roberto lifted his head and squared his shoulders. With Andrea at his heels, he walked into the small living area, smelling the saltiness of a pasta sauce brewing. His father was lazing on the bench, reading the Italian newspaper. His mother came out of the kitchen and gave Roberto a hug, the aroma of fresh basil strong around her.

She broke from the hug. "How was your first day at work, darling?"

Roberto shrugged. "Fine, Mama." He looked at Andrea. "Andrea's invited me to go to his place for dinner. Can I?"

"But darling, I've made your favourite orecchiette pasta. Don't you and Andrea want some?"

Andrea shook his head. "It's okay, Mrs Morandi. We'll probably have the same sort of thing at home, but thanks anyway."

Her eyes darkened. For a moment, Roberto was afraid she would make him stay here and eat dinner with the family. Then she said, "Okay Roberto. You can go, but don't stay too long."

Roberto nodded and rushed out before she could change her mind.

Chapter 2

DISCOVERY

R oberto and Andrea walked around hilly slopes and along cracked walkways, as the old ladies of the village gawked in their direction. The wind grew chilly with the approach of evening. Shadows deepened in the dimming light.

As they entered Andrea's home, Roberto smelled freshly baked bread, and something else he couldn't put his finger on. The house was cosy but small, with a balcony, three bedrooms, a spacious kitchen that featured pots and pans hanging from the ceiling, and a rug-filled living room with antique furnishings. His own mother's pots and pans were dented and scratched, looking nothing like the shiny, reflecting surfaces of these pots and pans. Roberto felt almost at home in this house.

This kitchen was as big as his whole house, and it made him wish for more. If only he could have nice things for once. If only they could live in a large house like this one. Maybe one day, his father would do well in the business.

Andrea's father, Salvatore, was sitting at the oversized timber top table, watching a television program with his housekeeper, Rosa, a short chubby woman who had been a part of the family since Andrea's mother had died two years prior. Rosa got up from the table, and ushered Roberto in. Salvatore smiled briefly, then turned back to his show. Rosa gave Roberto a kiss on both cheeks. She then grabbed both his hands and rubbed them gently. She smelled of fresh lavender and pasta sauce. She'd always been caring—like a mother to Roberto.

"My dearest Roberto. How have you been?"

"Good, thank you. And you?"

Rosa's eyes turned for a moment. "Well, you know, cooking some lasagne. I had a feeling you were coming for dinner." She smiled. "We also have freshly baked bread. Take a seat, dear. Dinner is almost ready."

Roberto nodded, and Andrea grew quiet. They waited at the table while Rosa took the lasagne out of the oven and placed it on the stove. Then she began slicing the bread, which smelled delicious.

Andrea's father owned his own bakery in the main centre of the village, and worked there with his employees who worked various shifts. He worked for most of the day, sometimes rising early to get the bread ready for customers.

Roberto excused himself to go to the bathroom then headed upstairs. When he came out, he heard muffled voices by the balcony. He tip-toed closer to the balcony without being noticed, and watched as Andrea and his father stood deep in conversation. Salvatore towered over his son as if Andrea was a lowly ant. Salvatore's eyes were focused, his lips pursed. He shook his head vigorously. Roberto heard his own name and edged closer. His breathing shallowed.

"You should think long and hard about this," Salvatore said.

"But Papa, Roberto is my friend—and Giovanni is a good man. Please don't say such things. They surely don't deserve it."

Salvatore's brow furrowed and his fists clenched. He inched closer to his son, as if he was about to strike. "You shut your mouth." Andrea said nothing. "Do you hear me?"

Andrea shrank away from his father, who must have taken his silence as defiance. Salvatore's hand shot out and struck Andrea forcefully across the cheek. Andrea winced. Tears welled up in his eyes, and he pressed a hand against his reddened cheek.

Breathing heavily, Salvatore turned and stormed off.

Roberto was lost. He had to leave. How could Andrea's own father have hit him like that? He had no right, for Andrea had done nothing wrong. Roberto ran down the stairs and met with Rosa who stopped him in his tracks.

"Roberto dear, where are you going? Dinner's just about ready."

He was breathing hard, and thought his heart might stop. "I'm sorry, but I need to go. Please tell Andrea that I'll speak to him tomorrow."

Rosa shook her head. "Nonsense. You shall do no such thing. Now, sit."

Roberto caught his breath and listened for the others.

Salvatore and Andrea returned and sat down at the table. As if unaware of the tension in the air, Rosa served up the plates and smiled, then settled herself in another room to eat. The poor woman couldn't even eat with the family, and she'd lived with them for two years. Roberto shook his head and wondered, as he did every time he joined Andrea for a meal, why she wasn't treated like part of the family. It seemed like Salvatore's money hadn't made him a better man.

Andrea ate slowly, his head bowed and his shoulders slouched. Salvatore watched with darkened eyes, then turned towards Roberto, and said,

"So how are your parents?"

Roberto swallowed his pride. "Good, thank you, sir."

"Great to hear." Salvatore seemed to look straight through him. "You tell your father I'll be buying some wood for the bakery. I'll come by tomorrow."

Roberto nodded. "He'll be happy to hear that. Thank you."

He took a bite of the soft, moist lasagne. The salty sweetness of the mince sauce was almost enough to make him forget his sense of unease. It was heaven to taste. Not like the watery soups he ate at home.

Andrea stared into his food and remained silent.

When they finished their food, Salvatore called out to Rosa. She came in, still chewing, wiping crumbs from her mouth.

"Please wash up," Salvatore said. "I have a guest coming for coffee within the hour."

"Of course Mr Adessi."

He nodded and turned to Roberto with a sardonic smile. "Give my regards to your father."

Later that evening, Roberto stopped outside his house and caught his breath. He closed his eyes and thought about his dear friend, Andrea. How long had Salvatore been treating him this way? What had Salvatore and Andrea been talking about? There was something about his father that Salvatore didn't like. But what? Salvatore had always been pleasant towards his father, and was buying wood from him, but something else was going on. Maybe Salvatore was thinking of helping his father build the business. Mama always said Papa wasn't a good businessman. Maybe Salvatore was afraid he'd lose money if he went into business with Roberto's father.

As he turned to go inside, he heard hurried footsteps. Andrea was running towards him, gasping for breath.

"Wait up! I need to talk to you."

Roberto crossed his arms. "What's wrong? You couldn't talk to me at the house?"

Andrea shrugged. "You were weird today. With my dad, I mean. What's going on?"

Roberto angled his head. "I saw something today."

Andrea frowned. "What?"

Roberto took a deep breath and clasped his hands as if in prayer. He couldn't meet Andrea's gaze. "I saw your dad slap you."

Silence surrounded them for a moment, and Roberto wondered whether he had done the right thing. Maybe he should've just spoken to his Papa.

"No big deal. I can take it." Andrea shrugged again. "It's nothing. Nothing."

Roberto nodded, unconvinced. "Has he hurt you before? Those bruises, I mean?" Andrea said nothing. "Andrea, please tell me the truth. Maybe I can help you."

Andrea laughed. "It was just a slap. We had an argument, that's all. My dad looks out for me—doesn't like me going out on my own much. He worries. Thinks there are bad guys out there."

"Bad guys?" Roberto's cheeks warmed. "I heard my father's name mentioned."

Andrea sighed. "Like I said, Roberto. It didn't mean anything." An awkward silence prevailed for a moment. "Anyway, I'd better go. My dad thinks I'm in my room."

Roberto watched him leave, then stepped inside the house, lost in his own thoughts. His mother came to meet him. There was no sign of his father. He must be in their room.

"Did you have dinner, darling?" his mother asked. "Would you like some food?"

"I ate at Andrea's. I'm not hungry." Sluggishly, he walked towards his bedroom to prepare for sleep. He only wished he could have a gourmet meal like lasagne every night.

Chapter 3

BLESSINGS

R oberto stepped out into his parents' vegetable garden the next day. It was cloudy and misty with a sharp, chilly wind. He stood cross-armed and watched his parents fill a sack with olives, freshly picked from their tree. Three more large burlap sacks sat on the ground, bulging with olives. When all the sacks were full, Roberto helped his father push them into the house and downstairs into the cellar. His father smiled and patted Roberto on the shoulder.

In a breathless voice, he said, "So glad we can finally sell our olives at the market. We'll make a bit of money there, Roberto." His father clasped his hands to his chest and let out a long breath.

Roberto nodded and returned the smile, proud that his father could make some extra money from their home-grown fruits and vegetables. After working so hard to grow them, Papa deserved it.

Roberto's limbs felt light. He almost wanted to dance. Smiling broadly, he followed his father outside, then headed over to the vegetable patch, where a wooden edging kept the broccoli, brussels sprouts, peppers, and spinach contained.

His mother was picking vegetables, bending over with a sigh as she wiped her brow with a soggy handkerchief. Roberto picked up a handful of sacks and went to gather the vegetables, making sure they weren't mixed, but sorted by type. He looked over at the pears and prickly pears that his father was sorting, and continued to help his mother.

Roberto's feet sank into the wet grass. He tipped back his head and smelled the fresh, damp mist, heard the sounds of donkey steps in the distance, and his father's heavy breathing as he worked. Maybe his father wouldn't need to work as many hours selling wood. Maybe they would finally have the money to get some decent Christmas presents. Life would be easier for a while.

Once his mother had picked all the vegetables, she let out a huge breath and smiled at Roberto. "So much food, darling. This'll bring in some good money for us."

Roberto tapped his foot on the ground. "I can't wait, Mama. You both work so hard."

His mother grabbed her handkerchief and wiped her forehead again. "We all work hard, son. Don't you forget that."

"Okay, Mama."

Roberto tied up the burlap sacks, and his father helped him carry them inside. He looked over at the rusty barn, surrounded by cobwebs and dust, with a cracked corner window. The barn stood lopsided from wear and tear, and was already filled with tools and other equipment for their woodworking, so there was no storage space for the vegetables and fruits.

As he and his father were about to head back outside, a knock at the door stopped them. His father answered the door. It was Salvatore. Roberto stiffened and pressed his lips together, then remembered that Salvatore had mentioned he'd be stopping by for wood. Roberto peered around his father and their guest and saw Salvatore's car parked, shiny in the mist.

Salvatore barged into the house with his head held high. Roberto wondered about the gleam in his eyes as he shook his father's hand and said, "Good to see you, Giovanni. I've come for more wood."

His father didn't meet Salvatore's gaze. "There's some in the barn. I'll get it."

Salvatore greeted Roberto then turned to his father. "So, I see you've got all your supplies for the market. Good work."

Papa didn't answer but just walked out through the open door and headed for the barn, his back stiff and straight. Roberto always wondered why his father and Salvatore weren't friends. There always seemed to be tension between them.

Roberto's mother approached, and Salvatore's face reddened. His mother shook hands with their guest. "Can I get you a coffee, Salvatore?"

His eyes seemed to light up. "No thanks, Maria. I've just come for the wood—I—I have to get back to the bakery."

Papa came out of the barn, carrying a crate of wood. The veins in his neck stuck out, and Roberto wondered if it was the weight of the crates putting pressure on his neck.

His father set the crate at Salvatore's feet while money was exchanged. He noticed Salvatore pulled a few bills from his pocket and threw them at Roberto's father. "Oops, sorry about that. It slipped out. I must have butterfingers."

Papa cleared his throat. "It's okay."

Salvatore bent to give Mama a lingering kiss on the cheek. Mama blushed. Papa crossed his arms in front of his chest, but said nothing. Something was wrong, but what? Just a friendly kiss on the cheek. There was nothing unusual about that.

Salvatore said goodbye and winked at Roberto. "See you at home, Roberto. Andrea would love to see you soon."

Roberto nodded. "Sure, I'll come by." As he watched Salvatore load the wood into his Fiat, an uneasiness settled over him. He brushed it off and got back to work in the garden.

He thought about the slap and considered telling his father, but what good would that do? Fathers and sons occasionally had fights. Just because his own father had never slapped him, didn't mean that others didn't.

Later in the day, Edoardo, Filippo, and Angela ran into the house and threw their backpacks on the ground. Their parents were sitting at the kitchen table, enjoying a cup of espresso while Roberto looked in the kitchen drawer for some glue for a woodworking project.

Edoardo spoke first. "Why are you guys all so tired?" His lanky figure hovered over Roberto as he helped him look for the glue.

His father beamed. "Oh, son. We have our beautiful vegetables to sell. Some extra money finally coming in."

Angela hugged both her parents. "That's exciting. We'll sell each one."

"That hardly ever happens," Filippo said. "We've always had leftovers."

His father's joy was contagious. "Not this time, son. We'll get to have a nice Christmas and sell a lot more this year. We've earned it."

"We sure have." Roberto finally found the glue, and headed to his father.

He forgot all about Salvatore and their struggles with money. This year would be a great year; a year filled with joy and lots of presents. Finally, his father was smiling again

Chapter 4

SUPRISE VISITORS

A week later, on a wintry Friday, Roberto woke up to the sounds of his parents' voices in the kitchen. He opened his eyes and rubbed them hard, feeling as if pins were pressing into his eyelids. His stomach churned as he pondered last night's nightmare about Andrea and his father. He'd had other dreams this week, and fatigue set in from broken sleep.

He thought about Salvatore slapping Andrea, and wondered if there was more to it than just the slap. Yet, how could he get Andrea to be honest about it? How could he help him? It wasn't like anyone would believe that Salvatore would hurt his son, at least intentionally. Salvatore was one of the wealthier businessmen, well-respected in the community. No one would believe a twelve-year old boy over a man who had brought in a respectable service to the small town of Eboli.

As he was rising from bed, his parents came into the room. His mother sat on his bed. She took his hand and smiled. "Darling Roberto, how about you come into the city with us?"

Roberto rubbed his eyes. "Too tired. I'd rather stay home." He looked at his father. "What's going on today?"

"Well—your father and I have to go into the city for supplies for the business— you know, some more wood and crates, and a few other bits and pieces. Will you be okay the whole day on your own?" Mama stroked his cheek.

"We'll be back soon," his father said. "We'll be stopping in at a few places. Maybe you can do some woodwork."

Roberto nodded. "Okay."

"Now listen," his mother said. "Don't leave the house. Just stay inside. No-one will bother you. The others have already gone to school."

Roberto rubbed his brow. "I'm not a baby."

"I'm sorry, darling. I know that. You just take care." She kissed him on the cheek, and Papa patted him on the shoulder.

He lay there for a while after his parents left, blinking the cobwebs from his mind. A whole day, all to himself. He threw back the covers and stretched, then went into the kitchen, sat at the cracked and weathered table and had sweet homemade cake and milk for breakfast. The cake's aroma had a citrus smell and was still warm from the brick oven his mother had made it in that morning. It was the one special treat they could afford. He had a shower and thought about his day. His father had some woodworking tools in the barn, so maybe Roberto could make a wooden car or bookshelf. He enjoyed doing things with his hands, and had the skill for it. His father had taught him. Maybe in the future he could start his own business or build houses. He knew he didn't wish to sell wood for the rest of his life. Not that he was ashamed of his father, but Roberto wanted more from life. Papa never had the opportunities that Roberto could eventually have if he was smart about it. He could potentially secure a future in carpentry or building.

After his shower, Roberto stepped into the tool barn and grabbed all the tools he'd need to make the wooden car. Papa had bought him the materials back when he'd first expressed an interest in making one. The car symbolised movement, ambition, and drive, and it would take him to places he'd never dreamed of.

Roberto started sawing plywood, and then attached pieces together with glue and a nail gun. He found some rubber to use as the fake tyres and shaped them into solid, round spheres. Once these were glued to the car, he painted the wood a dark brown. His father had recently bought plastic, so he used that for the side windows and the windshield. Then he left the car to dry on large pieces of newspaper. He sighed with relief at a job well done, and decided to reward himself by sitting outside to watch nature and the birds soaring.

Sitting on a weathered cane chair, Roberto breathed in the fresh smells of trees and mountain air, and the smell of burning wood. Nearby, crickets chirped and frogs croaked, while in the distance, a rumble of thunder warned of a coming storm. The clouds were grey, and the wind made him shiver. He loved and hated this season because he enjoyed listening to the rain, but loathed the Christmas tradition of never getting the gifts he wanted. He knew his parents were doing the best they could, but if only one year he could get whatever he wished for. If only, he could afford to buy something for his siblings and parents. Maybe, one day.

Footsteps on the cracked pavement snapped him out of his reverie. Roberto stiffened in his seat when he saw two robust men walking towards him. One man had prominent dimples on both cheeks, while the other had dark, almond-shaped eyes, and towered over his companion. They looked threatening. An uneasy feeling settled in Roberto's stomach. What did they want, and why were they approaching his house? Were they after his father? Were they friends of his parents? He'd never seen them before, and didn't think that men who appeared so intimidating would be friends with them.

He hurried inside and peered through the curtains, waiting for a knock. What should he do? He knew his parents weren't expecting anyone.

A heavy knock sounded on the door. Roberto held his breath, heart pounding.

He hesitated and opened the door slightly.

A gruff voice called, "Hey there! We know you're inside. We're friends of your father's. He told us to come by to help him out with his business."

Was it true? Could his father have forgotten he'd invited visitors?

The knock came again. This time, Roberto opened the door a crack. The two men were standing side by side, grinning. The tall one said, "You must be Roberto. He's told us a lot about you. Is he home?"

Roberto shook his head.

"We've got a list here of some men he can approach for business. Might be able to get him selling some other equipment for us. You see, we've got a company selling lots of different products, and we want your dad to promote them. We'd pay him for his travels, and in return, he can sell some of our products."

Roberto frowned, considering their offer. It sounded great. Papa could make a lot of money by doing this. Surely he wouldn't pass on the offer.

"I can let my Papa know, and tell him you stopped by."

The shorter man with prominent dimples said, "That'd be great. We—aah—heard that you make some great things with wood too. There might be some business in that. Can I take a look?"

Roberto was suddenly excited. His heart almost skipped a beat. "Wait here. I'll bring them out to you." Realisation suddenly hit. "How did you know about my interest in woodwork?"

The shorter man said, "Your father told us. Like we said, he talks about you a lot."

The tall man shifted from foot to foot and blurted. "Can I use your toilet? Long trip, and all. We've walked so long, and I really need the bathroom."

Roberto hesitated. He didn't know these men. They were strangers, but they might be his father's friends. He couldn't be rude.

"Okay then." He hoped he was doing the right thing. His mother had told him to stay inside.

He swung open the door wider, and both men entered the house. The shorter man followed Roberto into the tool barn. He showed the man his wooden car that was still wet from the paint.

His face lit up. "This is amazing. We could really sell these kinds of things."

Roberto was laughing on the inside. "You think so?"

The man peered at his solid gold watch. Roberto thought he must really be making money, to afford that watch. "I know so. What else can you make?"

"Bookshelves, boxes, crates, you name it. I can make it." The man nodded and looked at his watch again. "Why do you keep looking at your watch?"

"Force of habit, I guess. There are always deadlines to meet so I keep track of time. So show me what else you have."

Roberto directed him to a bookshelf filled with knick-knacks of all sorts, pencil cases, tables, and miniature puppets made of wood. He was proud of his collection. It represented their hard work. His father had a talent for making things but had never had the opportunity to use his talent.

"Anyway, tell your father that we'll drop by next time about the business."

Roberto had a spring in his step. "Sure thing."

He was drumming his feet against the floor, whistling. He was waving his arms, using grand gestures. He felt alive.

This was their chance. The chance to make money, and lots of it. They could have a real business for wealth instead of survival. They'd never struggle again.

As they both walked back inside, Roberto noticed the other man was missing. "Where's your friend? Does he usually take this long in the toilet?"

A sudden noise came from the back of the house. Roberto turned, and the dimpled man grabbed his arms and twisted them behind his back. Roberto gasped. "What are you doing?"

He struggled to break free, but the man yanked his arms upwards. He cried out as a searing pain tore through his shoulders.

"Hurry up, will you?" the man growled to his companion. "I can't hold him all day." The tall man came into the room, twisting a piece of rope between his hands. While the dimpled man held tightly to Roberto's arms, the tall man looped the rope around his wrists and knotted it tightly.

"Sorry to do this, but I have no choice." The dimpled man pushed him towards a closet filled with blankets and sheets. He opened it and shoved Roberto inside, grabbing another piece of rope to tie him to a bar across the top of the closet. Roberto was stuck inside.

He felt sick. "Why are you doing this? What do you want?"

The man closed the door without answering. Roberto was enclosed in total darkness. His breathing became shallow as he struggled to untie himself. He tugged at the rope, groaning in exhaustion and pain as the rope cut into his wrists. A warm wetness trickled down his hands. It was useless. The rope was wound too tight.

He heard doors opening and closing and something heavy being dragged across the floor. Eventually, he heard the sound of a trotting horse. Or was it a donkey? What was going on? Why had these men really come here? To rob them? Why choose a poor family to steal from? These men weren't Papa's friends, so how had they known about Roberto's woodworking? Had someone put them up to this? There had to be a reason.

Chapter 5

LOST HOPE

Time passed. Roberto's wrists burned and his shoulders ached. His parents would be home soon, and then the pain would end. Then he'd see the disappointment on their faces, and he'd have a different kind of pain. Why, oh why, had he opened the door for these men?

By the time he heard his brothers' voices and his sister's high-pitched laugh, he'd lost the feeling in his hands, and his cheeks were crusty with dried tears. He heard the smack of the front door opening, and the thump of backpacks dropping to the floor.

He moved his mouth but no sound came out. He swallowed hard and licked his lips and tried again. "Help! Help me!" It was a whisper. His vocal chords felt dry and shrivelled.

Through the crack where the door met the floor, he watched their shadows pass as they laughed and teased each other on their way to the kitchen for their after-school snacks. He imagined how it would be. Angela preparing dinner while Edoardo and Filippo did their homework.

This time, he kicked the door and screamed until his throat was raw. "Help! Help me, please!"

The chatter stopped abruptly. The closet door swung open, and Angela was looking down at him. "Oh my God! Roberto!" She came towards him and fumbled with the knots that tied him to the bar. "What happened to you? Who did this?"

While Edoardo crowded in behind her, Filippo hurried to the kitchen and came back with a knife. "Hold still," he said. "I'm going to cut you loose."

When Roberto was free, and they'd rubbed the feeling back into his wrists and shoulders, Edoardo sat back on heels, his forehead furrowed. "Were we robbed?"

"Yes, I think we were robbed. I just don't know what they took?"

He told his siblings about his visitors. Filippo shook his head, pointing his finger. "Why would you let strangers into the house, Roberto? You know Mama and Papa would have a fit if they found out."

Before he could answer, the front door opened. His parents stepped into the house, carrying bags of groceries and other hidden items. His mother hefted a large bag that held a lot of products.

Both his parents approached them in the living area, staring at their children in confusion.

"What happened here today?" his mother asked. "Roberto?"

When Roberto didn't answer, Filippo explained what had happened, while Edoardo watched with crossed arms and Angela made a quick exit to the kitchen to cook dinner. Roberto's hands felt clammy. Why did she leave? He needed all the support he could get. No doubt, his parents would punish him for letting strangers inside the house? He should have just spoken to them outside and asked them to come back when his father was home.

Roberto watched as his parents stepped out of the living room. They both shook their heads and headed downstairs to the cellar to check if anything was missing. He jumped when he heard a scream. It was his mother's voice, and for a moment his heart almost stopped. He raced to the cellar, his brothers and sister thundering behind, and saw his parents lowering their heads, his father placing his hand on his mother's shoulders. They seemed to have aged ten years. His siblings stopped and huddled nearby, looking confused.

His father shuffled closer to Roberto, and asked, "Tell me your version of events about today, Roberto."

Roberto held on to his stomach, and then slowly explained everything.

Giovanni's shoulders slumped. "How could you let this happen? This was a lifetime's worth of supplies—now gone. Don't you see? The one business is never enough. This was our lifeline and now we'll continue to struggle, continue to be poor. They even took the money we had saved from the trunk. How could you let this happen?" He sighed heavily and broke eye contact.

His mother looked haggard. Tears squeezed from the corners of her eyes. "We trusted you Roberto, and now this. How can we survive now? This was my idea, and now it's all gone. All gone." His mother left without turning back to Roberto. His father rose, and walked upstairs.

Filippo left without a glance at Roberto, while Edoardo and Angela looked concerned.

"Don't worry too much. We'll work something out, don't worry," Edoardo said.

"Of course we will. You hang in there, and we'll come up with a solution. There's always a solution to every problem," Angela said while touching him on the shoulder.

When Edoardo and Angela had gone, Roberto covered his face with his hands, and then walked through the room. All of their fruits, vegetables, and sacks of flour had been taken. Dust marks on the floor showed where the crates had been. All those months they had scraped and saved, eating as little as they could just so they could grow the produce and buy the flour to make bread. Now, because of him, all that hard work was wasted. His stomach clenched. How would they survive now?

Giovanni picked up a block of olive wood and ran his hand across the grain. He was doomed in business. He'd always known that, but he hadn't expected this from his son. The son he trusted not to let strangers into the house. No doubt, Maria would blame him for this too. He never seemed to be good enough for her. Where was the intimacy they once shared?

He had hoped that, once the vegetables sold, he would finally gain Maria's approval and possibly even Salvatore's. He knew she compared the two of them in business, that she saw Salvatore as the more successful man. Maybe Giovanni wasn't ruthless like Salvatore but at least he had a measure of values he lived by. He loved his family, and had always promised himself that they would be taken care of, even if it meant burning himself out.

Now, though—now it was gone, and with it, he felt the chances of winning his wife's admiration slipping away.

He held up the block of wood. It was a beautiful thing, cut from the heart of an olive tree. He closed his eyes and saw the thing he would make of it. A heart-shaped jewellery box with a velvet lining. Something special to surprise Maria with. All his love, he would pour into it, and the moment she saw it, she'd know what was in his heart. He opened his eyes, and saw where he would make the first cut.

Chapter 6

JOINT DECISION

The next morning, Roberto rose from bed and dragged his feet. He'd had a bad night's sleep which left him feeling lethargic and worn. Still yawning, he put on his slippers and shuffled to the kitchen, where he poured milk over stale bread and carried it to the table. He sank into the chair and looked at his breakfast, but he had no appetite. His shoulders ached, and the rope burns on his wrist still stung. As he pushed the mush around with his spoon his father came in, and without even looking at Roberto, warmed up some milk on the stove. The sadness in Papa's face as he brought his mug of milk to the table made Roberto's throat tighten.

Avoiding Roberto's gaze, Papa said, "Don't worry about coming in to work today. I'll be fine on my own."

Roberto drew back. "But—it's my job now, Papa. I want to help."

His father shook his head and slid into the chair across from Roberto. "I'm not very busy today, so don't worry. Stay home with your mother. She might need you to run errands for her."

Roberto's shoulders slumped. He swallowed past the lump in his throat and said, "What kind of errands?"

Papa shrugged. "You'll need to ask her that."

Eyes burning, Roberto looked down at his sodden breakfast. He had ruined everything.

Giovanni couldn't bear to look at his son. He knew the pain in Roberto's face would make him weak, but there was more to it than that. Maybe his son's poor judgement yesterday reminded him of his own failings. Maybe it was only disappointment that, once again, his plans had come to nothing. Perhaps it wasn't entirely Roberto's fault. He was just a boy after all. Yet, he had lessons to learn. Giovanni wanted his son to grow up with a stronger instinct than he had. Roberto couldn't just let strangers inside the house. Particularly when he couldn't defend himself.

The thought of what might have happened made Giovanni's mouth dry. What if the strangers hadn't been satisfied with locking Roberto in the closet? What if they'd decided to do worse? Maybe even silence him for good? He realised his hands were trembling and set his cup carefully on the table. What a foolish, foolish thing his son had done.

Giovanni thought about calling the police, but why bother? The Italian police had bigger fish to fry. They'd never catch whoever had stolen the family's livelihood. It would never be a priority case for them. Even if the men were caught, the family would never get their supplies back. Besides, these men were most likely long gone by now.

Still something niggled at Giovanni. Why target a poor family? Why not go after a wealthy household? It didn't make sense.

Roberto's mother entered the kitchen. She kissed him, then Papa on the cheek, and gave Roberto a reassuring smile. He summoned the courage to speak.

"Papa—I——want to say I'm so sorry about yesterday. Those men. They seemed okay, and I—I didn't think they would do that—and I want to help you. In any way I can."

His father covered his face with his hands. Roberto's nails dug into his palms. Had he caused this? Of course he had. It was his fault that his father looked ten years older than he was overnight. Papa didn't speak nor did he look at his son. Taking a last sip of his milk, he grabbed a piece of bread, rose from his seat, and left without a word.

Roberto's eyes burned, and he turned away from his mother. Sick to his stomach, he bowed his head. He couldn't bear to see his father like that. He'd always wanted to please his father, honour him, and stand by him. He never wanted to put added stress on him, but now he had failed him.

His mother walked up to Roberto. She pulled him close and hugged him, then stroked the back of his head.

"Oh, Roberto, my darling; Just give your father some time. It's a matter of pride. It's not about you but—his need to take care of his family. He feels he has failed us, and cannot bear for us to struggle any longer. Just give him time. Be patient. He will come around, you will see."

He pulled away from her embrace, lowering his head. "But I'm the one that failed him, Mama. Not Papa. It was my big mistake, and I promise that I will fix this in some way."

His mother nodded. "Your father loves you, and he knows you'll learn from this mistake. We can only be there to support him. Can you give him time?"

Roberto nodded. "Yes, Mama. I can do that." He forced a smile. "Now, what can I do for you today?"

His mother pondered. "Well, I will need some bread from Salvatore. What we have is a bit stale."

"Of course, Mama. Would you like me to go now?"

"They won't be open yet, but I'm sure you could go to the house and spend some time with Andrea. You must miss him terribly."

Roberto did miss being with his friend, talking to Andrea and having lunch together.

From the hallway, he heard his brothers and sister teasing each other.

"I will go now, Mama. I'll see you soon."

"You sure will, my darling. Give my love to the family."

Roberto set off with his knapsack and headed out of the house. It was a short walk to Andrea's house, and he wanted to make sure he had time with his friend before school started. He often thought about school, but his father needed him, and that was how it was meant to be.

At least, it had been before he had destroyed his family's future. Would Papa even want his help now? He had wanted to go back to school, but not like this. Not because he had let his family down.

He strolled along the path, turning his head up to watch birds fluttering in a flock. A cool breeze brushed his cheek. The weight of his father's disappointment grew lighter as he drank in the beauty of the distant hills, the towering trees and rows of stone houses. As he passed through the village, lines of damp clothes stiffened in the cold while dust particles swirled in the wind. An elderly woman washed a shirt in a tub of water, while a donkey hovered near her shoulder. She gave Roberto a toothless smile, seemingly oblivious to the smell of nearby donkey faeces. Roberto held his breath and hurried past.

He reached Andrea's house and knocked. A moment later, Andrea swung the door open, and a broad smile brightened his face.

"Roberto, my man. So good to see you. What are you doing here?"

Roberto entered. "My Mama wants some bread, and I thought we'd catch up before you went to school."

"Sure thing. Just having breakfast. You want some?"

Roberto shook his head, even though the saltiness of fresh, fried eggs and the delicious smell of bacon made his mouth water.

Salvatore was sitting at the breakfast table while Rosa served him. They both waved, but Salvatore's eyes narrowed briefly. What was that about?

"Come, have breakfast, Roberto," Rosa said.

"No, I've had breakfast already, but thanks." He turned to Salvatore. "Oh, by the way, my Mama would like to buy some bread. I have the money here."

Salvatore nodded. "Of course, Roberto. I'll get you some as soon as Andrea gets off to school." He shot Roberto a sharp glance. "How's your father doing? With the business, I mean?"

Roberto's stomach turned, but he kept his voice steady. "Fine sir. All good, thank you."

Salvatore clapped Roberto on the back. His grin came a beat too late. "No need to call me sir. Call me Salvatore."

"Okay." Roberto waited for Andrea to finish his breakfast, then they walked to Andrea's bedroom. Roberto sat on a desk chair wringing his hands, and Andrea sat stiffly on the bed.

"What's wrong?" Roberto asked. "You look as if you're in pain."

Andrea crossed his arms. "Nothing. Just hurt my back playing soccer the other day." He stared into the distance. "Anyway, I should be asking you the same thing. You look like someone died."

Roberto couldn't lie to his friend. He explained what had happened with the strange men.

Andrea frowned. Then his eyes brightened. "Listen, I've got an idea. Wait here." Roberto's stomach fluttered. Could Andrea help him? Was there hope, after all? He clutched at his chest, and held on to a sliver of hope. He waited with bated breath until his pulse raced. What was Salvatore doing here? Was he going to help Roberto's family?

Salvatore gestured for Roberto to leave the room with him. "Let's have a private talk, just you and me."

Roberto's breathing quickened, and he followed Salvatore's lead. They walked into a large storage room that contained a small timber desk, oversized plastic storage boxes, a cast iron bookshelf, and three armchairs. Salvatore sat on one of the armchairs, and motioned for Roberto to sit on the other, facing him.

"So—my son tells me that you've had a robbery. He said that two men took your savings and food supplies. Is that correct?" Roberto nodded, feeling numb. "Well, I'm happy to help, but—,"

Roberto took deep breaths. "But what?"

Salvatore pursed his lips. "Well, your father is a proud man. He may not want my help. Maybe I can tell him that it'll be a loan. He can pay me back with no interest. How does that sound?"

"I don't know. Like you said, my father probably won't like it. He—he feels like he has failed his family, and this might make things worse."

Salvatore touched his temple. "I understand, but I also understand that he has scraped and saved for all these supplies. They even took money, didn't they?'

"Yes, sir. I mean—Salvatore."

Salvatore waved his arms expansively. "Your father hasn't failed. He succeeded by being able to save all those supplies. To be able to save all that money." He took a breath. "I believe that your father has his pride, but he also wants to do the very best for his family, isn't that right?"

Roberto nodded. "Yes, that's right. He wants us to have the best."

"And I can provide that." Salvatore's gaze was penetrating. "Like I said, it'll be a loan. That way, he will have the control to pay me back at his leisure. No extra payments."

"Thank you, sir. I mean, Salvatore. It'll really help. Thank you so much." Warmth radiated throughout

Roberto's body, and his heart raced. He jumped out of his chair, and shook Salvatore's hand. It was finally happening. They were saved.

Chapter 7

A HELPING HAND

Two days after his conversation with Salvatore, Roberto lay smiling up at his bedroom ceiling. He wasn't sure when Salvatore planned to speak to his father, but he hoped it would be soon.

Filippo came into his room, and said, "What are you smiling about?"

Roberto glanced up. "Nothing."

Filippo sat next to him on the bed, sighing. "Listen, Roberto. I know you feel bad about letting those men in, but I'm sure you learned your lesson. It could've been worse." Roberto scooted into a sitting position as Filippo wagged a finger at him. "You need to remember though, that life's not about chasing your dreams. It's about practicality. You've got to think about providing for this family. Then an incident like that will never happen again."

Roberto's chest tightened. Heat flushed through his body. How dare Filippo judge him this way? He cared about his family's future but he also wanted to follow his own dreams. Didn't he have a right to that? It was the promise of more money for the family that had tempted him to open the door. A small voice inside him said it hadn't been as simple as that. Hadn't he been flattered when the man complimented his woodwork? Hadn't he really been following his own dreams?

What if he had? Didn't he have a right to that? If only Filippo understood him. If only Filippo understood that life wasn't only about pleasing others, but pleasing yourself too. He brushed away his thoughts when his mother called out to both of them.

As he swung his legs over the side of the bed, he heard voices in the living area. Sullenly, he walked into the living room with his brother. His heart pounded when he saw Salvatore waving his hands in the air. The big man stood near the sturdy wooden bench in front of Roberto's parents, who were sitting on cane chairs. Angela and Edoardo sat on the sturdy wooden bench, looking up at Salvatore with curiosity.

Roberto and Filippo took their places on chairs near the kitchen and waited. Salvatore held his hands loosely behind his back, his eyes scanning the room.

"I wanted you all to be here for this, so I'll get started." His eyes fixed on Roberto as he continued. "Roberto explained the situation with the robbery, and I wanted to offer you some money."

Papa turned away and shook his head. Mama frowned.

"Cool," said Edoardo.

"That's very generous of you, Mr Adessi," said Angela.

Roberto's mother turned to his father, laying a hand on his shoulder. His father rubbed his arms and looked the other way.

"Exactly how much are we talking about, Salvatore?" Mama asked.

Salvatore's eyes lit up. "Whatever you need. We can discuss that later, in private." Turning to Papa, Salvatore said, "And what are your thoughts, Giovanni?"

Giovanni rubbed his temples. Who was this man, questioning him this way? He had honour; he had dignity. Why couldn't Salvatore discuss this financial situation in private? Why was he putting on a show with all the children? They were too young to be involved in such things.

Giovanni watched the way Salvatore stared at Maria. It was unnerving. His penetrating eyes made it obvious he was still infatuated with her. How dare the man behave that way?

Giovanni was the one who had won Maria in the end. He was the one who truly stole her heart. He thought of the way she had looked at him when he'd asked her to marry him. Her eyes were filled with love and pride. It was true. She had loved him then but it had been a long time since she'd looked at him that way.

Turning away from Salvatore he said brusquely, "We're fine thanks. We don't need any help."

Salvatore gave an easy nod. "We know what a great provider you are, and—bear in mind, it'll be a loan. You can pay me back without interest." He leaned forward. "I'm in a great financial position. The bakery's doing well and I have some other side businesses that are successful, so I'm therefore in a position to help you. This money I give you won't affect me at all."

How dare this man come waltzing in here, gloating about all his businesses? Hadn't Giovanni been shamed enough? He didn't want to choose between his pride and his family. No doubt Maria would think differently, but pride was important to a man. "I said, we don't need your money."

Maria laid a hand on his arm. "But darling, think of the children. Forget about your pride. We can pay Salvatore back. Won't you feel better about that?"

The silence was thunderous. Giovanni couldn't bring himself to speak. While he gathered his thoughts, Salvatore turned to Roberto. "What do you think, Roberto? Do you agree with your father?"

Roberto wanted Salvatore's help, and he wondered if he could convince his father. He understood it was a matter of pride, his father feeling defeated by this. Papa seemed to have grown smaller. Yet, this was all his fault, not his father's, so he had to take a stand.

Roberto rose and walked over to his father. He knelt and touched his father's shoulder. "Papa, this is all my fault. I was the silly one who let those men in— even when I felt that something wasn't right. I still let them in— all because of my own selfishness. Please don't let my mistake cost you. You work so hard, and we all appreciate that. We can do with a little help."

His mother said, "We'll be able to buy some nice presents for everyone."

Roberto held his breath, waiting for his father.

"I don't think so," Papa said.

Salvatore said, "I can leave and let you discuss this as a family. No pressure, but as I said, Giovanni, you are a great provider for your family." As he turned away, Mama rose and touched his shoulder.

"Wait! Don't go." She turned to Giovanni. "What do you say, darling? Your family must come before pride."

"Papa, please accept it. Let's have a nice Christmas," Roberto said. His siblings joined in.

"Yes, Papa. Everyone needs help from time to time," Angela said.

"We want this," Edoardo said.

"It is very practical, Papa," Filippo said.

Papa's gaze roamed the room, as they all waited for a response. He stared down at his hands. "Fine, we'll accept your offer—but I will pay you back."

"Excellent." Salvatore leaned forward and held out his hand. After a moment, Papa shook it.

As his children leapt up, laughing and chattering among themselves, Giovanni's heart broke. What was his pride compared to his family's happiness? Yet how could a man live without pride? Such a small thing, wasn't it? Accept a loan, and suddenly, magically, all their problems were solved. What did it matter if Salvatore was the hero? Surely Maria and his children would understand the sacrifice Giovanni had made.

He would simply work harder, so he could pay Salvatore back. Hopefully with his pride restored.

Salvatore left, but Giovanni still felt flat. His head felt heavy and his chest tight. While his family happily planned how they would spend the money, Giovanni left the room and walked to his barn. A sharp pain shot through his chest. He pressed a hand to his heart until the pain subsided, then drew in a deep breath and picked up the heart-shaped box.

Chapter 8

NOSTALGIA

Maria was watching Roberto and Giovanni load up the donkey for the day's work. Her husband slouched and avoided her eyes as she said goodbye. Roberto shrugged with a frown. The grey sky loomed, and Maria felt the damp mist in the air as she stood outside, watching. A steel tub of clothes lay in front of her.

She thought about her husband and how his pride had almost stopped him from accepting Salvatore's money. He had to think of the family and not just his pride. The time was ripe to start providing for them. God forbid if her neighbours ever found out they'd been robbed and were accepting a handout from the town's most powerful business man.

If only Giovanni was able to use his artistic skills for profit. He was a great woodworker and craftsman, but his attention to detail didn't allow him enough time to custom make for a profit. Instead, he'd made wood pieces in his spare time and as a hobby. She hoped Roberto had more of a head for business as he too was skilled with woodwork.

Maria thought about Salvatore and wondered how her life would have been different if she'd chosen to marry him. They'd had a brief relationship when she was eighteen, but by the time she was twenty, she had met Giovanni at church and fallen madly in love. For a while she'd struggled to leave Salvatore. He'd showered her with gifts and was a true gentleman. He was charming and highly attractive, and she knew without a doubt that he'd be a good provider if they were to marry and have children. Did she love him? She didn't think so at the time, and while she had her doubts about Giovanni's monetary acumen, she was in love and thought that was enough to have a decent life together.

Maria's father was patriarchal and didn't approve of Giovanni, stating, 'He's a lowly craftsman and will not provide for you'. He would've preferred that she marry Salvatore. Once she'd chosen to marry Giovanni her father had cut off all contact. Since her mother had died when she was five years old, the loss of her father had been doubly hard on her. In the end, Salvatore became possessive, and she wasn't comfortable staying in the relationship anyway.

His attempts to control her, the way her father had, made the decision that much easier.

Maria returned to the present and wrung a tea towel into a steel tub. She hung it on the clothes line outside the house, careful not to drop any clothes onto the dirt. As she was hanging a pair of pants on the line, she felt eyes on her. A sweet, musky smell penetrated the air, an aftershave that was familiar.

Looking up from the washing, her heart fluttered. What was that about? She saw Salvatore strut towards her with a wide smile. His strong gaze made her draw back.

He held out a piece of paper, and she put out her hand to retrieve what looked like a cheque.

Maria swallowed. "It's only been a few days since we talked. There was no rush for this." She pocketed the cheque.

"Nonsense. It is absolutely my pleasure to help you, Maria. Always."

She grabbed a linen blanket, wrung it, and hung it on the line. "Thank you." She felt herself blush. Her mouth suddenly became dry, and she could hardly catch her breath.

"I'm just wondering if I could trouble you for a cup of tea?"

Maria's heart raced. "Of course." She finished the last of the clothing, and was about to grab the tub when Salvatore reached for it. "Thank you," Maria said.

"I am always happy to help." His gaze unnerved her so she turned away.

They headed inside the house. Maria started filling up a saucepan with water, then grabbed tea leaves. His presence behind her gave her a lightness she hadn't felt in a long time.

Setting down the cup on the table, Maria sat across and watched him sip his tea. He was still as handsome as ever and hadn't aged much at all in the past twenty years. She lowered her eyes. Why was she thinking about his good looks when she had a perfectly loving husband? It wasn't right.

Salvatore said, "I wanted to talk to you about Giovanni."

Maria winced. "What?"

Casually, he unbuttoned the top button of his shirt, exposing the hollow of his throat. "I just wonder how married life is these days."

Maria shook her head. "It's all good. Why do you ask?"

He leaned in, resting his forearms on the table. "We haven't spoken in a while—and I wanted to see how you were doing. How family life is."

What was he really asking her? They'd lived in the same village all these years, so why was he asking now?

"We're doing fine, thank you. If it wasn't for that robbery, we'd be just fine. That just set us back a little, that's all. It can happen to anyone."

"Of course. But misfortune happens to some more than others."

Maria scraped a hand through her hair. "I guess you're right?"

Salvatore's eyes held hers. "And it is unfortunate that Giovanni has had to struggle. I know he works hard to provide for you and your family, Maria."

Maria turned away, and rubbed a hand against her heart. Why was she feeling things that had lain dormant all these years? His penetrating gaze struck her, and it took her back to the way he'd kissed her all those years ago. How he had made her feel things that were out of this world. He had pleased her in many ways—his charm, his touch, his booming laugh. How her skin had warmed at his touch, and her whole body thrummed with a thousand tiny vibrations. With Giovanni it was different. He had also pleased her, but Salvatore was lustful and exciting while Giovanni was generous, heartfelt, and calming. She'd had an adventure with Salvatore, but with Giovanni she had a security she could never get with Salvatore who was much too possessive for her liking. She could never live like that.

"I guess we all work hard. You do too."

He nodded. "If you ever need anything, financial or otherwise, please don't hesitate to call on me. Come to the bakery." He smiled. "I haven't seen you there in a while."

Her heart skipped a beat. "I'll try my best."

Salvatore rose. "Just tell me one thing."

"What?"

He reached over and touched her on the shoulder. "Do you ever think about all we've been through over the years? Our struggles and our losses?" Maria remained silent. "Without my wife, it's been hard, lonely even. I really miss her, and I also recall—our time together. They were adventures, weren't they? Good times."

Maria's stomach did a little flip, but she brushed it off and edged away. "I liked your wife. She was a great lady."

Salvatore nodded, then stared at her for a long moment before strolling out.

What was this magnetic pull towards him? Whatever it was, she didn't want it.

Chapter 9

PRIDE

When Giovanni and Roberto returned in the early afternoon, Maria was cooking bread soup, adding a touch of seasoning to the water. Edoardo, Filippo, and Angela weren't due from school for a couple of hours yet.

Giovanni kissed Maria on the cheek as she faced the stove. Roberto hugged her from behind. The wood crackling in the fireplace created a nice warmth in the kitchen.

"Can I go to Andrea's place?" Roberto asked.

Maria turned her head for a moment. "Of course darling, but make sure you're back in time for dinner."

"Okay, Mama. See you both later."

Roberto rushed out of the house with a smile.

Maria turned off the gas and set aside the soup, then joined her husband on the sturdy wooden bench. He was resting his feet on a foot stool when he spotted the cheque on the table.

"What's this?" he asked.

"Salvatore dropped that by today."

His fist clenched. "He came here when you were alone?" Maria nodded. "Why would he do that?"

Maria shrugged. "He had some spare time, so wanted to drop it by."

Giovanni got up from the couch and stood near the table. He looked down at Maria who suddenly felt exposed. Yet that was ridiculous. She had nothing to hide. She'd done nothing wrong.

She lifted her chin and said, "Why don't you tell me what's really on your mind?"

"Nothing." He sighed and crossed his arms. "I guess we have the money. That's fine." Maria rose and stood close to him. "Well, I think it's great what Salvatore did. He only wants to help."

"Of course he does." He gave a wry laugh. "I guess we'll be better off now. So what did Salvatore have to say? Did he come inside?"

"He had a cup of tea." The muscles around her husband's eyes tightened.

"I see."

"He invited himself in," Maria added.

Giovanni sighed again. "What's done is done. I have something else to discuss with you." He fidgeted the way he always did when he had to give her news she wouldn't like. Her stomach did a slow roll. What now?

Giovanni looked into his wife's face and saw that look that said she was anticipating bad news. The furrow between her brows, that slight tilt to her head, her eyes wide and wary. She was still so beautiful after all these years. In spite of their difficulties, he was more in love with her now than he ever was.

Before he could speak, she clasped her hands. "What is it Giovanni?"

"I saw your father in the city today. He said he'd be dropping by."

Maria drew back. "What? Why?"

Giovanni shook his head. "Maybe he wants to make amends."

"After all these years?"

Giovanni shrugged. "He was talking about Salvatore and how lonely he was, now that his wife's no longer alive. They met in the bakery." He tried to keep the resentment from his voice. "I know your father's never liked me. I wasn't his preferred choice for you, but—"

"But what?"

Giovanni blew out a long breath. "Nothing."

Maria rose from the couch and slipped her arms around him. She smelled of soap and lavender. "Come on, you can tell me anything. I love you."

Giovanni's heart warmed. That was all he needed to hear. He turned into her embrace and wrapped his arms around her, but their moment was interrupted by a knock on the door.

Maria pulled away and headed to the door, wincing at the sight of her father outside. He was a short man with stubble on his chin, grey-black hair, and a stocky build with a protruding belly. His eyes were cold and hard.

"Well, aren't you going to let me in?" he said.

Maria shook her head. "You haven't changed, have you? After all these years you're still a miserable old man."

A muscle in his jaw pulsed. "Is that any way to talk to your father?"

Giovanni walked over and pushed the door open further. "Come on in."

He got a grunt from her father, Luigi, who avoided Giovanni's eyes and stalked in to sit at the kitchen table. As the old man's gaze swept the room, Giovanni was suddenly aware of the worn table and the modest furnishings.

"So I saw Salvatore, and he's doing pretty well for himself." Luigi stared at Giovanni hard. "It was a shame about his wife dying like that. Such a shame!"

Giovanni wanted to punch him, but he respected his wife too much for that. How dare he boast about a man who had the morals of a leaf?

Maria stood at the table. "Why are you really here? What do you want?"

Luigi's eyes smouldered. "Can't a father visit his only daughter?"

Giovanni noticed Maria's teeth clench. "You haven't visited in ten years," she said. "Ever since Edoardo was just a baby. You don't even know what they look like now, do you?"

He nodded. "I've seen them in the village. I have kept tabs on them."

Giovanni took a seat at the table while Maria made coffee and served up brioche. As her father devoured it, she poured coffee into a cup with shaking hands, almost dropping it on the table. Her father frowned but then his expression softened. Giovanni felt a glimmer of hope. Was this old man suddenly realising the error of his ways?

"Look, I just want you to be happy." His gaze flicked to Giovanni and back to his daughter. "Are you happy, Maria?"

"Father, I love Giovanni with all my heart. We've made a nice life together." He gave her a shrewd look. "Yes, there have been financial difficulties, but we survive."

"I'd like to offer you some money. Salvatore explained what happened to you, and it's devastating."

Giovanni spoke up. "We're fine."

Maria said, "Salvatore helped us out."

Luigi nodded, a hint of a smile at the corners of his lips. "He mentioned that."

Maria put her hands on her hips. "Like Giovanni said, we're fine. We've got by without your help for all these years. Why would we need it now?"

Luigi glanced away, blushing. He rose and cleared his throat, then gave Giovanni a brusque nod. He faced Maria. "Please come and visit me. I haven't moved."

As soon as the door closed behind him, a sob burst from Maria's throat. Giovanni took her in his arms and stroked her hair. "It must've been hard for him to come here. Why don't you try to sort things out? Maybe visit him with the children one day."

"We'll see, darling. We'll see."

He broke away from her. "Don't lose contact because of me. I don't want that for you."

Giovanni knew that despite her angry words to Luigi, Maria admired much about her father, and that this loss had hurt her deeply. It bothered Giovanni that her choice to marry him had cost her her father. The man challenged her in a lot of ways. She could never get his approval, but all her life she tried her hardest to get it. If only she could prove him wrong about their marriage, then maybe the relationship could be restored.

Giovanni looked at Maria, stroking her cheek. He wiped away the tears, then kissed her gently on the lips. As the kiss became deeper, he took her by the hand and led her to the bedroom. They had time before the children got back.

Chapter 10

LETTING GO

G iovanni looked out of the window of the bus, smiling to himself. His eyes turned to Maria and his children, chattering and laughing about their fun day at the beach. It was an hour's ride by bus, and Giovanni had decided to take his family out and share some news with Roberto.

The sun's glare warmed his face and heated his whole body, helping him relax. This trip would provide a much needed escape from his business.

Watching his family, a dull pain spread through his chest. It hurt that Maria had been more relaxed and light-hearted ever since Salvatore had given them the money. Giovanni wanted to be the one who made her feel relaxed and carefree. It shouldn't have been Salvatore coming to the rescue, like a knight in shining armour.

At the thought of Salvatore, a sour taste filled Giovanni's mouth. If Maria had married the baker, she would have had a life of ease. She would still have a relationship with her father. No more struggles about money. Yet, would it have been a better life?

Giovanni thought about the love they'd known when their life together was still new and they were doing well. After the war, like many families, they'd fallen on hard times, and their financial woes had permeated their relationship. These past few days, he'd felt the tension lift, seen something of the old love in her eyes. He would do anything to fan those flames again.

He needed to stay afloat, needed to repay his debt to Salvatore, and sustain his financial freedom. Otherwise, he would've lost his pride for nothing. He felt torn. He knew Maria loved him, but he also knew she was attracted to Salvatore with all his grand schemes and financial success. Obviously Salvatore still carried a torch for Maria too. Was that why he'd offered the loan?

Giovanni felt a grudging gratitude towards Salvatore. How ironic that his rival may have given him the very tools he needed to rekindle the passion in his marriage. He wanted more for his family, and hoped that with the money he had sacrificed his pride for he could put more of the lightness in their lives.

Giovanni closed his eyes momentarily and breathed in the fun-filled chatter from his family. He'd always wished to provide more for his family, but hard work alone didn't seem to be enough. Salvatore had it easier coming from a wealthier background. However, there was more to it than that. Salvatore had a ruthlessness that served him well in business, a ruthlessness that Giovanni had never been able to cultivate.

Giovanni broke off his thoughts when the bus came to a stop at the beach. He rose from his seat and grabbed his beach tote and towel, heading outside. His family followed behind, pushing him and each other along in their eagerness to reach the shore.

Giovanni waited for Maria as the children ran towards the sand and settled their bags and towels. Edoardo jumped into the shallow water near the shore. Roberto started to take off his shirt, and Filippo arranged his towel on the sand. Angela was yelling at Edoardo to stop splashing her.

Giovanni loved seeing them excited this way. He thought again of his plan to make more money. It meant initial sacrifices, but in time he'd get a good return. He couldn't wait to tell Roberto.

He took in the crowd on this warm day, lying underneath umbrellas, scrounging for seashells, licking ice-creams or biting into a brioche. The raspy wind brushed his face and filled his nostrils with the salty air.

Giovanni and Maria settled onto a towel while the children played in the water, rippling with small waves in the low tide.

Maria turned to him with a reassuring smile. "When are you speaking to him?"

Giovanni looked into her eyes, realising how lucky he was to have her.

"As soon as he gets out of the water."

She nodded, then grabbed his hand. "It was a great idea coming to the beach. The kids are enjoying themselves. Thank you, darling." Maria leaned forward and pecked him on the lips. He stroked her face.

"Have I told you how much I love you?"

She chuckled. "Not lately, no."

"Well, I do. And—"

"And what?"

He averted his eyes. "This decision I've made will help Roberto in the long run. He'll provide more for the family with his wits about him."

Maria held his hand against her cheek. "What you're doing is a huge sacrifice, but I'm sure it'll all work out."

Giovanni nodded as all the children rushed out of the water and grabbed their towels, water dripping onto their bags.

"I'm starved," said Edoardo.

Roberto frowned. "You're always starved. It's still too early for lunch."

Edoardo shoved him and messed up his hair.

Filippo shook his head "Do you always have to act like a clown, Edoardo?"

"And do you always have to be so serious?"

Filippo huffed. He sat on the towel next to his mother, who patted him on the back.

Angela took out some bread and handed it to Edoardo then took a sip of water from a bottle.

"I'm going for a run," Edoardo said.

Maria looked concerned. "You can't run on the sand, darling."

"I'll just be over by those trees. There's a track over there." He grabbed a pair of runners from a bag and put them on. "I have to practise for the school running team."

Maria reached over to Edoardo and patted his shoulder. "I'm so proud of your ability. All those trophies you have."

"Thanks, Mama."

Edoardo set off with Filippo and Angela. Roberto was about to follow when Giovanni rose from his towel and touched Roberto on the shoulder. "Let's go for a walk. I need to talk to you about something."

Roberto looked curious. "Sure, Papa."

They strolled towards towering trees, passing a group of people on picnic blankets, sharing espresso coffee in minute cups. Then, finding a tattered seat, they sat side by side and watched passersby. The sounds of babies crying, waves crashing, and motorbikes in the distance were welcome distractions. Giovanni turned to his son and patted him on the shoulder with a smile.

"I think you should go back to school."

Roberto's mouth dropped open. "What?"

"I'll be fine in the business on my own. I have some new ideas, so I think you should return to school. Be with Andrea."

Roberto broke out into a wide grin and hugged his father. Giovanni was touched that he could do this for his son. It had been selfish of him to take him out of school in the first place. Now he had to think of his son. He would manage without him.

Roberto broke away. "But, Papa, I thought you needed the extra help."

"It's all good, son. I have a plan, don't you worry."

"What, Papa? What plan?"

"I've decided to custom-make some of my woodwork. Some people in the community have asked me to make them bookshelves— and other things for their homes. It will bring in extra money."

Roberto nodded. "That's a great idea, Papa. Thank you."

Giovanni patted him on the leg. "I'm happy that you'll be finishing your education. You'll make me proud, Roberto. I know you will."

The joy in his son's eyes warmed Giovanni's heart. He grabbed Roberto's hand and they headed back to the family. Yes, he thought. It was all going to be okay. He felt it.

Chapter 11

DEVASTATING NEWS

Three weeks after the beach trip, Roberto and his father were in the barn making a bookshelf for a friend. Giovanni hammered nails into a plank of wood, joining it with another piece. Roberto held on to the pieces of wood, sighing as he watched sweat bead on his father's pale forehead. Papa was looking tired and weak lately, working extra hard to pay back Salvatore's money.

Even though Roberto was now back at school, he still had to think of a way to help his father more. Papa barely had time to sit and relax. All he did was travel widely with his business and work the market to sell their newest crop of fruit and vegetables. Roberto helped at the market, selling beans, potatoes, corn, and grain for flour, and he'd recently helped to grow grapes to make wine. He worked on crushing the red grapes and placing them in barrels to ferment the wine. Only recently, his father had sold some of the wine.

No matter how hard Papa worked with the wood business and the markets, they were only barely surviving. Post-war, a lot of the people couldn't afford to pay top prices for food and wine, so his father was forced to keep his prices low just to make a pittance from the sales. Several times, Roberto had woken up in the middle of the night to find his father busily tapping away with his tools.

Roberto knew it was a matter of pride and shame to take Salvatore's money, so Papa wanted to restore his pride by paying him back quickly. However the pressure his father was putting on himself was taking its toll. Roberto was beginning to worry.

His father finished hammering then grabbed sandpaper to sand down a new piece of wood. He looked up at Roberto who was sweeping up pieces of wood on the floor.

"I appreciate your help, son. Thanks."

Roberto turned to his father. "I'm glad to help, especially when you're working so hard. Can't you slow down a bit?"

His father stopped sanding. "And why would I do that?"

Roberto was careful with his words. "Well—you've been looking really tired lately. I think you need more rest, Papa."

His father continued to sand down the wood. "The quicker I get things done, the quicker I get paid. Then I can pay Salvatore back. It's a win-win for all of us."

"Not if you make yourself sick."

"I'm fine, Roberto. Just fine."

Roberto stood still for a moment. "But Mama told you the same thing. Why won't you listen?"

Giovanni looked up again. "Oh, stop fussing and get back to work. This is my choice, Roberto. I'm fine."

Roberto grabbed a brush and pan, sweeping up the dirt and wood and placing it into the rubbish bin. He walked over to the bathroom to wash his hands, then returned to the work room.

Papa had his back turned towards him, but he was unusually still. He had stopped sanding. As Roberto approached, he saw that his father's hand was pressed hard against his chest. His eyes were half-closed.

"Papa? Papa, what's wrong?"

His father's breathing was shallow. "Call—your—your—Mama."

Roberto bolted from the room and headed to the kitchen where his mother was cutting carrots.

"Mama, something's wrong with Papa. Come."

Her eyes widened. She dropped her knife and ran with him to the work room. Papa lay crumpled on the floor. With a frightened cry, Mama ran over to him and pressed her fingers to the side of his neck. "Thank God!" She sighed with relief. "He has a pulse, and he's still breathing." She turned to Roberto. "Listen, go call the town doctor. Do you know where he lives?"

"Yes, Mama. I'll go now."

She nodded and knelt beside his father, stroking his cheek. "It's okay, darling. You're going to be fine." Roberto left and ran faster than he'd ever run before.

When he returned to the house with the doctor, a slim older man with a bald patch, the man rushed to Papa, muttering a quick greeting to Mama. He checked Papa's pulse, and did some other tests. A few minutes later, Papa was able to sit up. The doctor helped Papa to his bedroom while Roberto followed, waited, and watched. The doctor placed his stethoscope against Papa's chest and listened. He shook his head and turned towards Roberto's mother, who stood beside the bed, her hand over her mouth. She was barely breathing herself.

Edoardo, Filippo, and Angela tiptoed into the room. Filippo headed to his mother and held her hand.

The doctor took a breath. "It seems like Giovanni's had a heart attack. His heart is very weak. I don't have the right medication or tests here to perform, so we'll need to get him to the hospital once he's stable. He's simply too weak to move right now." He looked at Roberto. "I could quickly go to the hospital now, get him the right medication which will hopefully stabilise him, then get the ambulance to pick him up. He'll need blood tests and a chest x-ray at the hospital.

His mother's eyes welled. "Yes, doctor. Please do that. You must save him."

"Let him rest for now. No undue stress."

She nodded distractedly, hardly seeming to notice when the doctor left.

Mama turned to Roberto. Immediately, she put her arm around him and Filippo. Angela and Edoardo rushed over to her, put their arms around her, then sat at the edge of the bed, watching their father sleep. He looked peaceful. Hopefully the doctor would return quickly.

Almost two hours passed, and still no sign of the doctor. Where was he? What was taking him so long? Could his father hang on until the doctor came?

Roberto held his father's right hand while his mother kept a strong hold on his left hand. Papa's eyes fluttered open, and he struggled to speak.

"Do you want to say something, darling? But you should really reserve your strength. The doctor will be here with the medicine shortly. You must hang on, darling. Please hang on." She turned her head away, but not in time to hide her tears.

Giovanni drew in a rattling breath. "Just one thing—to all of you. I love you all, and I—want you, Maria, to be happy if—if I'm not around."

"Please Papa, you don't need to talk," said Filippo.

"We love you," said Angela.

"Come on, Papa, you're a fighter. I want you to be okay so you can hit me with the wooden spoon. It's okay," Edoardo said with a chuckle.

Mama said, "Darling, we will be happy with you. Stop saying such things."

He ignored her and turned his head toward Roberto.

As Roberto approached, he saw that his father's hand was pressed hard against his chest. His eyes were half-closed.

"Papa?"

His father's breathing was shallow. When he spoke, his voice was almost a whisper.

"Promise me, Roberto. The woodwork—you love it. You'll continue to do that."

"Yes, Papa, but I will do it with you. Only with you."

His father shook his head. "No. Promise me."

Roberto's eyes hurt and his shoulders were in knots. He had a sick feeling in his stomach. "Yes, I promise, Papa. I love you. We all love you. Please hang on."

"And finish the—box. A gift for —your mother," Giovanni whispered. "In the room, you will find it."

Roberto nodded.

Silence penetrated the room as Papa became too tired to speak. His eyes slowly closed and his hand suddenly felt limp in Roberto's. He looked peaceful. He was just sleeping, wasn't he? Roberto called out to his father, but there was no response.

"Papa," Roberto said. "I am here. Talk to me please."

Maria bowed her head into her hands and wept.

Roberto glanced around. His brothers and sister were all crying. No, this wasn't happening. He shook his father's shoulder. "Papa, wake up. Papa, I am here now. I can run your errands. Please tell me what to do. Papa?"

He pressed two fingers to his father's wrist but there was nothing. He put his hand against his father's heart but there was no sign of a heartbeat. He pounded hard against his father's chest.

"Papa, please wake up. I am here now. I will take care of you. Please, Papa." Roberto laid his head against his father's chest. Tears streamed down his face. His mother stroked his hair, but said nothing. No-one said or did anything for a long time. Roberto felt like he'd been stabbed in the heart ten times.

The family sat huddled together near his father's still body, saying nothing. Roberto was in a daze, unable to believe his father was gone. His body felt dead but his mind reeled with many bad thoughts. Nothing mattered anymore, and he wanted to die himself. Why couldn't God take him instead of his father, an honourable man who didn't deserve to die so young.

Some time later, the doctor arrived, and sadly pronounced his father dead.

Roberto should've known his father was under a lot of stress, and it was his fault for not doing more to help him. Now, it was too late.

His mother kept his father's body in the house until the day of the funeral two days later. It was a sad affair with all the guests wearing black attire, and bringing flowers for the church. Roberto sat in the front pew of the church and heard the priest give the sermon. Friends of his father's had spoken about the kind and generous man Giovanni was and how he never hesitated to help others in need. He sacrificed himself to help others, and he never faltered in that duty. He would be terribly missed.

Roberto noticed the whiteness in his mother's cheeks. Her hands trembled. She dragged her feet, unable to speak to anyone. Edoardo bowed his head as he listened to the priest. Filippo stroked his mother's hand, trying to reassure her, and Angela sat next to Roberto, silently letting the tears out.

After the service, they watched as Giovanni was buried in the earth while his mother cried softly to herself. Filippo was there with his arm over her shoulder, trying to be strong for his mother. Edoardo was shuffling his feet, looking away while Angela shrank away to be on her own.

Roberto turned to notice that Salvatore and Andrea were behind him. Andrea waved, and Salvatore nodded as if to acknowledge Roberto's presence. He hadn't noticed them before, so they must've just arrived.

After the burial of his father and a solemn blessing and prayer, they all made their way back home on foot. The guests walked in a line and sang songs of praise.

Andrea approached, shuffling his feet in the grass. He touched Roberto briefly on the shoulder. The others moved on ahead of them.

"I'm—aah—so sorry."

Roberto searched his eyes. "Thanks."

Andrea held back tears as he ran a shaky hand through his hair. "Well, I guess—aah, we'll see you back at your place."

Roberto nodded, half listening. He felt as though he was in a daze. Nothing seemed to make sense anymore. "Sure," he said.

He watched Andrea walk back to his father. Salvatore was talking to Roberto's mother. He embraced her, then instead of letting go, held her by the shoulders for a long time. Roberto didn't like seeing Salvatore touch his mother.

He moved on ahead and walked back home with the guests. They were having a feast of homemade lasagne, buffalo cheese, sundried tomatoes with homemade bread, and roast beef. The whole town had helped make the feast, as on their own they couldn't afford to make such luxurious, delicious food. Yesterday, he would've loved this food but today he couldn't taste it. He had no appetite.

Roberto remembered his Mama telling him that his uncle would be coming for the funeral, but where was he? Did he forget it was today? Roberto couldn't remember the man, but his Mama told him he had once visited the house when Roberto was a baby. Maybe one day, his Mama would sort things out with her brother.

What was he going to do without his father? Who would teach him to make the right choices? Why was such a good man taken away from them so early? It was an unjust world and he didn't know whether he could forgive God for doing this to them.

Chapter 12

OFFERINGS

It was a Saturday morning, and two weeks had passed when Roberto walked the trail to a view of the Picentini mountains. He sat on the rough, hard ground. The vastness of the breathtaking scenery gave him clarity and a new perspective. He loved this place and wondered if he would ever leave it. Once, he'd taken a trip with his father to the Sele river, where Papa had told him that Eboli was the largest town in the region of Campania. It was a beautiful place, but the town had been destroyed by World War II. It would take a long time for Eboli to go back to its natural state, rebuilt back to its former beauty, or so his father said.

Roberto sighed and took in the vast sky, the people in the distance rushing on donkeys with a delivery of supplies, and the sea of houses all crammed together like sardines. He rubbed his hands together, feeling the sudden rush of a sharp wind in the air. He thought he heard footsteps behind him and turned quickly, but nothing was there. Strange! Was his father sending him a message? Did he believe in the afterlife? He wasn't sure.

Roberto quickly rose, grazing his hand on a twig. He sucked on the wound as he made his way back to the house, and on the way, he thought about his mother struggling with money. The only money coming in now was from the custom-made book shelves Roberto continued to make for the locals. He wanted to continue his father's legacy in woodwork but that meant late nights while he attended school during the day. Often, he was too exhausted to complete homework and school projects. It was time to make changes.

He arrived at the house to find his mother. She was baking bread in the kitchen. He heard her huffing as she pressed and prodded the dough with sticky fingers, wiping her forehead with a damp handkerchief.

Roberto approached and stood across from her at the table. She lifted her head with a reassuring smile.

"You're up early, darling. Is anything wrong?"

Roberto hesitated. His limbs felt heavy, weighed down with grief and worry.

"I have to talk to you about school, Mama."

She stopped kneading the dough and shook her head. "No, Roberto. I refuse to let you leave. We'll find a way to keep you in school."

He set his jaw. "No, Mama. We're struggling. The only way we can do this is to keep going with Papa's business. That'll bring more money."

She moved to sit in the chair, clasping her hands. "You're doing great work with the bookshelves. Let's see how that goes."

"But it takes me too long. If I wasn't at school, I'd get more things done, and that means more money. I can do woodwork and sell the wood and vegetables. It'll work."

Tears streamed down her gaunt cheeks. "No, Roberto. You're staying in school."

"It's okay, Mama. Please let me do this for the family."

His mother stared down at her feet, shoulders sagging. Her eyes looked empty, but he could tell she knew he was right. "I'm so sorry, my darling. So sorry you have to do this." Her voice broke.

Roberto heard footsteps and felt a presence behind him. He turned and saw Filippo in the doorway, looking concerned. "I have a solution," Filippo said. He knelt beside his mother and took her hand.

She blinked back tears and searched Filippo's face. "What are you talking about?"

Filippo grabbed the handkerchief and wiped away the remnants of dough from their mother's fingers, then brought her a glass of water and sat in the chair across from her. "I've been thinking about this for a while. I have a friend of mine who's going to West Germany for work. It's a great way for them to make money and help their families." He took a breath, rubbing his hands together. "I've decided to go there with him. To Frankfurt. That's where a lot of Italians are heading to for work. It's buzzing with immigrants working over there, and eventually becoming citizens. He said there are jobs in the banks, so I should be able to train there as a banker."

Roberto cocked his head. "That sounds exciting."

His mother laid a hand over her chest. "Nonsense, Filippo. You don't need to go there. You still have school, and you excel there."

He shook his head. "School for me is getting out of this place and making a real future. This country may be a republic now, but there are still many injustices. I'd like to make a future for us. I can send money each week from my job. That means Roberto can stay in school."

Roberto touched him on the shoulder. "No, Filippo. By the time you settle in and make money, it would take months for it to get it here. There's no time to waste. I still plan to leave school and help Mama."

Filippo shrugged and his mother rubbed at the dark circles under her eyes.

Angela burst into the kitchen and flung her arms around Filippo.

"What's going on?"

Edoardo soon followed as he rubbed his eyes. "Can't anyone get any sleep around here? What's happening?"

Roberto said, "Filippo's leaving us. Going to Germany for work."

"No!" Angela squeezed Filippo so hard he gasped for breath. "No, you can't go. What about us?"

Edoardo's eyes darkened for a moment. Then, he flashed a smile. He walked to Filippo and slapped him hard on the shoulder. "That's a good thing, isn't it? Teach him how to be a real man," Edoardo joked.

Filippo rolled his eyes. "Only you would say such a thing. Have you no manners?"

Their mother brought her hands together and chuckled as she stared at all her children. "I'm going to miss all of this. It's the only thing that's kept me sane since your dear father died."

Roberto went to his mother and stroked her hair. "We'll still be here for you, Mama—and Filippo can visit on his holiday. Isn't that right, Filippo?"

He nodded. "I'll visit as soon as I can save up enough money, but it might be a while. It depends on my wage." Silence pervaded the room for a moment. "I'll hopefully come back once we're doing okay."

Mama turned to Roberto. "You'll miss Andrea, though, won't you?"

He lifted a shoulder. "I explained things to him, and he understands. I told him not to say anything to his father, though."

"Good," said Mama. "The last thing we need is another loan from Salvatore. We can work this out on our own. It'll make us stronger—a united family. Thank you to both of you. I'm truly blessed to have you all in my life."

Roberto's stomach hurt and his mouth was dry. He was losing his brother and school at the same time. Yes, he would miss his friends, but he'd do this for his family. No sacrifice was too big or too small. He'd have pride in helping out his mother and bring her some comforts.

Chapter 13

LIGHT IN SHINING ARMOUR

A week later, Filippo left for West Germany. Maria was making panettone, her heart breaking at the thought of having one less child at home. Filippo was too young to travel to another country, but he'd be settling in and starting his new job in training. He was the one she'd thought most likely to stay in school, but he'd been willing to make the sacrifice. She was proud to call him her son.

Maria thought back to her times with Giovanni. She missed him terribly. He was a kind, generous man with a huge heart and many people loved him. She recalled the time he had thrown her into the sea with all her clothes on.

She'd just told him she was pregnant with Filippo. Their clothes were soaking wet, but they laughed and chattered, then made love under the stars. Her heart was filled with so much love, it hurt.

She remembered the way he used to wipe his mouth with a serviette; first his bottom lip then his upper lip, always in that order. It was a habit that drove her crazy, but now she missed seeing it.

There were other times he stood up to her father, professing his deep, abiding love for her. He wasn't intimidated by her father when it came to his love for her. He'd even given her the choice to forget about him if it cost her the father daughter relationship, even though she'd known it would break his heart. That was the kind of man he was.

Had she put too much pressure on him? She wished she could tell him how proud she was of him, and how hard he'd worked.

Giovanni had been on his way to starting out on a new venture through his woodwork. Perhaps Roberto could continue that legacy in honour of him. She was proud of both of them for having started on this new project.

Pushing away her thoughts, she finished cooking the panettone and set it aside. She needed to get out. A walk into the city was what she needed. Her feet seemed to carry her there of their own volition, and as she found herself pushing open the heavy wooden doors of the church, she knew it was where she'd needed to go all along.

Entering the church, she peered at the stained glass windows, the statue of Jesus, and the array of candles that brought her comfort. Passing by the long pews, she lit up two candles. One for Giovanni and one for her mother. As she found a seat in the middle and sat down, she glanced at the people entering the church. So many people. Her temples throbbed, and suddenly she felt overwhelmed. Maybe it was too soon for this. Her heart ached for Giovanni, wishing he was there to share the religious ritual with her. Pain filled her chest and her hands shook as she said a silent prayer in honour of Giovanni. She knew he was there with her and suddenly felt comforted by his memory. Thinking of him, she could almost smell him, the soothing scents of sawdust and sandalwood underlaid with the faint smell of sweat.

Footsteps behind her brought her up from her knees, and she made a sign of the cross and settled into the pew. Parishioners filled the aisles, searching for seats. She nodded a greeting to some of the women she knew but remained silent. Her mind was filled with her dutiful sons, Filippo and Roberto who were making huge sacrifices for the sake of the family. She blessed them with wholehearted gratitude.

The priest finally stepped to the altar and greeted the parishioners. His sermon filled her with a comforting presence, then she took the bread, gave thanks, and returned to her seat. Songs of praise distracted her from sad memories as she joined in the lyrics.

When the mass ended, she rose and headed outside into the city centre. She squinted in the blinding sunlight as she wandered past the shoe shop and grocery store. Others had just left the bus stop and walked past the small cinema. She saw the bakery where Salvatore worked and wondered whether to go inside. The store had a large open window with a view of people buying their bread or pastries. They entered and left with full bags. She noticed Salvatore talking to customers and bustling about, but he didn't see her. He was still a handsome man. Still able to draw in an audience. As he appeared to be busy, she thought it best not to disturb him.

As she started towards home, a rough masculine voice called her name. Her heart leaped at the familiar voice. She turned and smiled at Salvatore, who ushered her inside the bakery. Raising his voice above the humming sounds of the industrial machines, he called to one of his employees, then led her towards the back and seated her in a kitchenette half the size of the shop. Smells of freshly baked bread, sesame seeds, and spices filled the air. Two bakers were pressing flour into dough while another slid the finished loaves into large wood-fire ovens. They seemed oblivious to her presence.

Salvatore's hands were clasped in his lap and his penetrating gaze unnerved her. He sat across from her, but it felt like he was closer.

"So what brings you by?" he said.

"I went to church. I didn't want to bother you at work."

"Not a bother at all. It's good to have the break." His voice softened. "So how are you and the family doing after—"

Maria gasped. "Fine. All fine, thank you. How's business going?"

"Never better." He grimaced. "Keeps me out of trouble."

Maria chuckled and shifted in her chair. "Well, I'd best be going. You have work to do, and I'm keeping you."

He gestured her towards the seat. "No, no. Please stay. There's something I've been meaning to ask you—and I planned on coming by this week, but—I wanted to give you all some time to grieve. I only just found out myself from Andrea."

Maria's heart raced. "Found out what?"

"Well, Andrea told me that Roberto's leaving school to look after the business."

Maria nodded. "Yes, he's an exceptional boy."

"Maria, there is absolutely no need for him to leave school. I'd be only too happy to contribute financially. After all, Roberto's like a son to me. I admire his hard work and tenacity. Such a bright boy for a twelve-year old." He spread his hands, palms flat against the table. "Let him stay at school."

Maria crossed her legs and fiddled with a rosary bead pinned to her top. "I don't know, Salvatore. That's very generous of you, but I couldn't ask you to do that."

"Nonsense. You aren't asking, and it would be my pleasure." He turned away for a moment, looking into the distance. "In fact, if it's a matter of pride—there is one way we could keep your pride intact."

She tilted her head to the side and blinked a few times. "How so?"

Salvatore licked his lips and pierced her gaze with his own. A flutter in her heart reminded her of his charm and good looks. "We could get married."

Maria's mind reeled. "What?"

He took a breath. "We'd be a family and I'd share the expenses. That way, you wouldn't feel it'd be a handout. What do you say?"

Maria leaned away from him. The table seemed suddenly very narrow, as if the space between them had got smaller. "I'm flattered Salvatore, but I'm newly widowed and I loved my husband. I must honour him for some time."

There was a flash of disappointment in his eyes. "I understand, but at least let me help you financially." He leaned across the table and took her hand. "Giovanni was a good man—and you might never get over him. I understand that, but why should Roberto have to sacrifice himself when he can make a bright future for himself. He's quite the craftsman, but he needs to learn about the business of making a living with his craft. School can do that for him. What do you say? Will you let me help your son?"

She pressed firmly on her hands, then looked up. "I will pay you back somehow."

"Fantastic." He lifted up his hands and gave her a hopeful smile. "Maybe—after you've had some time, you might—might—reconsider the marriage proposal." He rose. "I will bring you a glass of port to celebrate. Wait here."

Maria watched him leave, noticing his taut muscles and solid build. No, she couldn't marry this man. Definitely not. She was still mourning her dear husband.

Chapter 14

COSTLY INCIDENT

Twelve months later – 1949

Roberto sighed and kicked a loose cobblestone. Andrea was sick from school today, and Angela and Edoardo went to a primary school in a different part of the village, so Roberto was walking to school alone. He held up his wrist, admiring the new gold watch Salvatore had given him for his thirteenth birthday. It flashed in the light, the most beautiful, most expensive thing he'd ever owned. He hummed a tune and thought about his custom woodwork business that brought in a little extra money. It wasn't a huge amount, but it was enough to help with a few of the expenses. He was sure his father would be proud of his new venture. After all, it was a venture they had started together.

A twinge of guilt shot through him. He was keeping his promises to his father by continuing his woodwork and helping take care of his mother. However, he hadn't touched the heart-shaped box. Papa had put so much into it, and it showed the best of his workmanship. What if Roberto messed it up? He imagined his hand slipping, the chisel in it cutting a deep gouge in the wood. No, he couldn't take the risk.

He missed his father more each day, especially the look on his Papa's face whenever Roberto showed him a finished piece of woodwork. The look showed pride and joy in the work. He remembered how his father often worked late in the night, and the strong smells of wood, dust, and sweat on his clothes. A workman's clothes, showing just how hard Papa had worked for the family.

Skipping along the track, Roberto pushed his backpack higher on his back. He felt weighed down by his school books. He looked down at his runners with the rubber splitting off and reminded himself to be careful not to trip. Small holes had started coming through the soles but his mother couldn't afford new shoes. The money they received from Filippo didn't cover all their expenses. Yet,

Roberto thought he could do some extra woodwork for his neighbours and earn enough to buy new shoes.

A flock of birds passed overhead and grey clouds shrouded the blue skies. A smell of oncoming rain and flashes of silent lightning spread throughout the sky. Roberto picked up his pace. From a distance came the low rumble of thunder. He wanted to get to school before he became soaking wet.

As he looked into the distance, his school came into view. Then he heard the rustle of bushes and the sound of approaching footsteps behind him. As he started to turn, two strong arms grabbed him from behind, pinning his arms to his sides. He fell back against someone who kept him in a stronghold and yanked off his gold watch. The metal grazed his wrist and the sharp sting made him gasp. As he tried to break the man's hold, he noticed a tattoo on his attacker's right arm. He'd seen that tattoo before, on one of the men who had robbed them of their fruit and vegetables. He flung his head back straight into the attacker's nose. The man moaned in pain and reeled backward. Roberto stumbled free and fell forward into the dirt.

"You idiot. You almost broke my nose." The man's voice was muffled by the balaclava that covered his face. For a moment, they glared at each other. Then the man bolted into the bushes.

Roberto panted, pushing himself up with shaky hands. Dust and dirt covered his clothes. He brushed himself off, torn between his desire to run for safety and his desire to go after the man and retrieve his watch. It was foolish to think he could overpower the larger man but the watch was the nicest thing he owned, and the thought of letting this man take it made Roberto seethe.

Then the brush parted and the man stepped out, holding a baseball bat. Roberto spun away, poised to run, but the man was faster. The bat came down hard against his right wrist. He heard the crack of breaking bones and a high-pitched scream that might have been his own as pain exploded in his wrist. He couldn't see. He couldn't breathe. He crumpled to the ground, hunched over his throbbing arm and waiting for the blow that would crush his skull. Instead the man laughed and ducked back into the bushes. Roberto retched and rolled onto his back, cradling his injured arm. The clouds were swirling in slow circles above him, the birds circling as if caught in a drain. He closed his eyes to stop the spinning.

For some time, he lay there on his back, drifting in and out of consciousness. Then he heard a car engine and a door slam. A voice that sounded far off in the distance grew closer and strong arms lifted him and carried him away. He smelled a familiar scent; a mix of wood cinnamon. He looked up, feeling drugged, as Salvatore laid him in the back seat of the car and covered him with a small blanket. "Just keep still, and don't move your arm." Salvatore closed the back door and got into the driver's seat. Roberto felt the car moving. Each bump in the road sent spasms of pain from his elbow to his fingertips. His whole body ached.

"What happened?" Salvatore said.

Roberto could barely speak. "A man—attacked—me. Took the watch."

Salvatore briefly turned as he drove. "It's okay. We'll get you to the hospital, have your wrist checked out. Not to worry, they'll take good care of you." He paused. "Did you see who it was?"

"No, he was wearing a mask." Roberto blinked back tears as the pain increased by the minute. "Which hospital? How far?"

"Soon. Just in Salerno. Hang in there, Roberto. You'll be fine."

Roberto closed his eyes for a moment, then had a thought. "What were you doing near the school?" No answer. "Salvatore? Why were you there? Aren't you usually at work?"

"I—I wanted to check on you. I know you usually walk to school with Andrea, so I thought you might want company. I obviously got there too late. I'm sorry, Roberto. Sorry I couldn't get there in time."

"It's okay. I'll live."

Salvatore chuckled. "Yes, you will live."

When they arrived at the hospital in Salerno, Roberto lifted himself up to see a sign saying Ospedale Via San Leonardo. He'd never been to this hospital, which was a tall rectangular building. As Salvatore drove along a narrow road, Roberto saw ambulances and smaller cars alongside a flat-topped grey building. A view of the mountain and towering trees were behind, the clouds grey with a hazy mist.

Salvatore stopped the car, then put an arm around Roberto, helping him walk to an emergency entrance. There he spoke to the receptionist, who instructed them to sit until a doctor was ready to see them.

Roberto walked slowly to his seat, the smell of disinfectant and smoke filling his lungs. Many people were sitting all around him, waiting, as he wondered when the doctor would see them. Groups of people were being called, and staff members moved in and out of the corridors and into small rooms.

He was tired, his wrist hurting. He tried to be brave as one person and then another was called. Others looked worse than he was, but he still wondered when it would be his turn. When Roberto was finally called in to see a doctor, a man with a beard and greying hair ushered them into a room and directed them to two chairs side by side. He sat across from Roberto and looked at his wrist, which had swollen to twice its normal size.

Roberto sucked in a sharp, whistling breath as the doctor pressed the wrist gently with his thumb and said, "It's hard to tell whether it's fractured—"

"Oh, it has to be fractured. Has to," Salvatore said. "I mean, with the amount of pain he's in, it has to be."

"Without an x-ray, I won't know for sure," the doctor said. He stood up. "We'll get an x-ray organised, then we'll know."

Roberto sat in the front seat of Salvatore's car, feeling flat. The doctor had given him tablets for the pain and put his arm in a temporary sling to keep the wrist secure, but nothing more could be done.

Salvatore turned to him. "It's not that bad, Roberto. The fracture will most likely heal with no need for surgery. You have to be patient and not do anything that will risk a further fracture. You heard what the doctor said."

"But I wanted them to fix it. Now I can't do anything."

"You can still go to school, but you'll need to learn to write with the left hand. I can help you with whatever you need. I'm here for you, Roberto. You know that."

Roberto shook his head and looked through the car window, feeling sick in the stomach. Why had this happened to him? Would he even be able to sand the furniture? Salvatore acted as if it was no big deal. Why couldn't Salvatore understand?

Chapter 15

PROPOSAL

Maria drew a hand through her hair as she pondered her current troubles. He mind took her back to Roberto's injury. She had reported the incident to the police but nothing came of it. She'd even asked Salvatore for help, and he'd used his connections to try to find the perpetrator, but with no success. He was the one who had brought Roberto to the hospital and paid for medical expenses. That was two months ago, and now, without Roberto's help from the custom-made side business, they were again struggling financially. With the right buyer, the stolen watch might have brought enough to carry them for a while, but it was gone and the attacker had disappeared.

She didn't know where to turn. She was tired of breaking her back, growing produce and baking goods for the market. A friend of Giovanni's had taken over the wood business, but he wasn't turning much of a profit.

Poor Roberto could no longer do his craft until his right hand healed, and that could take months. Hopefully the fracture would heal in its own time, as the doctor had said. The injury was not severe enough for surgery.

Maria thought about Salvatore. How she wouldn't have been able to manage without him. He was a God-send, and helped her financially. He hadn't even asked for anything in return.

Her mind cast her back to the last twelve months with Salvatore. After Giovanni died, he'd come to the house to bring the children many gifts. He even bought them school supplies, stationery, and backpacks. Then he and Andrea started coming over for Sunday dinners once a fortnight, then it became every Sunday, until now he was coming over at least several times a week with Andrea.

Before Roberto's injury, Salvatore had helped set up the woodworking business by giving Roberto money for supplies and distribution. Without Salvatore's help, they wouldn't have been able to survive. He was an angel sent from heaven, and she'd be forever grateful for his generosity.

Maria was about to step into the shower when a knock on the door startled her. She quickly put her clothes back on and hurried to answer the door. Her heart raced when she saw Salvatore beaming on her doorstep. She smoothed her hair with her fingers. His own hair was wet, as if he'd just had a shower himself. It made him look younger and more handsome. Her body radiated warmth. What was happening to her? She couldn't be having these feelings. He was just handsome. Surely any other woman would respond in the same way?

Placing her hand on her chest, she smiled back and invited him in. All her children were at school, so she was alone. Was that even wise? A part of her enjoyed the adventure of having Salvatore to herself. Was she crazy, or had enough time passed since Giovanni's death?

She directed him to the couch, and they both sat with their legs touching. Her heart beat faster and her mind became too fuzzy for speech. Why did he have such a strong effect on her? How could she stop her body from responding?

Salvatore leaned forward with a penetrating gaze. "How's Roberto doing?"

Maria reminded herself to breathe. "He's managing to write with his left hand at school."

"And his hand? Is it healing?"

Maria smiled. "It seems to be. He's complaining less about the pain whenever he does something now."

"Well, let me know if he needs anything."

Maria turned away, unable to cope with his unwavering stare. No man should have eyes so luminous. She rose and walked into the kitchen, then poured some homemade grappa into two tiny glasses. She carried them back to the couch and handed him one. He gulped it quickly, then laid it on the coffee table. She drank hers down, enjoying the strong, sharp taste, as strong as brandy. It made her body warm.

Salvatore touched her shoulder. "Maria—I know that things have been hard. I mean, ever since Roberto had his injury." He took her hand. "It breaks my heart to see you—well, struggling. You don't have time to just enjoy life."

"I'm fine, Salvatore. Besides, you've helped so much." She looked away. "I don't know how I can ever repay you."

He smiled, his eyes lighting up the room. "I don't expect any repayment, Maria. I hope you know that." He turned away momentarily. "I see you working so hard, and I wish I could do more to help."

"There's no need. You've helped so much already."

The intensity of his gaze made Maria's breath catch in her throat. "Maria—it's been a year now since your loss, and I—I—was wondering if—if you'd reconsider my marriage proposal. I can provide for you and your family, and you won't ever have to struggle again."

Maria felt butterflies and a tingle in her heart. Her tongue flicked across her lips. "I don't know, Salvatore. It's a kind offer but I'm not sure I can marry again."

He looked away for a moment. "It's no longer a scandal Maria, to live your life. To move forward. Giovanni would sincerely want that for you. To love again, be happy—be well-provided for. I know I can fulfil your needs if you just give me the opportunity. You don't deserve to struggle." He paused. "I know it's been difficult since Roberto's injury but I'm here to make your life easier. You know how I feel about you, and I hope you feel the same way." He looked deeply into her eyes. "I love you Maria, and I hope you'll do me the honour of being my wife. I will forever please you in every way possible." He took her hand and placed it against his lips. Then he moved closer towards her on the couch, leaned in, and kissed her slowly on the lips. Maria responded, breathless, wanting more. He embraced her and kissed her more deeply as their tongues met.

Salvatore broke away from her. "I'm sorry Maria. I couldn't help myself. I apologise if I've offended you in any way."

Maria felt her face flush. "No, it's fine."

He stroked her arm. "So—what are you thinking?"

She did feel something for Salvatore, and maybe it would make her life easier. She remembered his deep gazes at the kitchen table, wondering what it would be like to be in his arms. She remembered how he played bocce with all the children, making them laugh with his gestures and jokes. She thought about the time he'd tended to the wound when Angela had cut her ankle. He was there for her and her children in every possible way. Besides, Giovanni would want her to have a good life and move forward. He'd never want to see his family struggle in any way. Salvatore could make their dreams come true.

She nodded. "I'd love to marry you, Salvatore."

He rose, swooped her up and twirled her close to the couch, kissing her hard on the mouth. "I love you my dear Maria, and thank you."

They continued kissing until Salvatore broke away. Then he left with a bow. Maria was surprised with herself for agreeing to his proposal. A part of her was excited by such an adventure, and she knew she'd get that with Salvatore.

Chapter 16

WEDDING PREPARATIONS

As Maria was drinking an espresso, relishing her time alone while her children were at school, a knock came at the door. She finger-brushed her hair and pressed her dress smooth with her palms, thinking it was Salvatore. It had been a week since he had proposed, and she hadn't yet told the children about it. As she opened the door her heart missed a beat when, as she'd hoped, Salvatore presented himself there with a grin. He held something behind his back.

"I have a surprise for you," he said as he gave her a dozen red roses with a bow. She swung open the door and let him in. He grabbed her by the shoulders and kissed her, lingering.

"My goodness, you shouldn't have. Thank you."

Maria noticed his flushed cheeks and nicely-brushed hair. His shirt was open at the neck, exposing strands of hair on his well-tanned chest.

"That's not the surprise."

Maria was curious. "Then what?"

"Come on, let's go. Have you finished your coffee?"

She nodded. "Would you like one? I have some left in the pot."

He shook his head. "No, we have no time to waste." He took her by the hand. "I'd like you to see something special, and we have a bit of a drive."

She grabbed her bag, and they set off for a drive in his burgundy Beetle. They got into the car, and opened the windows to clear the stuffiness of the interior.

Salvatore wouldn't tell her where they were going. She was intrigued. These were the adventures she liked, and the ones she'd never had with Giovanni. Not that she didn't love Giovanni with all her heart or enjoy their life together, but Salvatore was of a different nature entirely. She wasn't accustomed to these adventures anymore.

Salvatore was driving a bit too fast for her liking, but she enjoyed the quiet as they passed the towering trees, swerved around curves in the mountain road and hummed through farmland with herds of sheep and grazing cows.

The sky was as blue as she'd ever seen it, and the sunshine cast a soft glow across Salvatore's face. He focused on the road, casting an occasional uneasy glance in her direction. What was he hiding, and what was he nervous about?

After driving for thirty minutes, they finally reached their destination. She saw that they'd reached Piazza Alfano and looked up to notice the Duomo, or Cathedral, in Salerno. What were they doing at the church? Was a mass in procession? She'd never been to this church but had heard amazing stories about its historical life.

They stepped out of the car in front of the cathedral, and she noticed the bell tower high above. Walking closer to the church, she gasped at its beauty and magnitude. It outshone everything else in the city.

Closer to the entrance, she saw its bronze doors with a multitude of panels featuring crosses and stories from Jesus' life. In the middle was a fountain surrounded by a variety of plants and flowers. The entrance had a portico with twenty-eight antique columns, and pointed arches.

She turned to Salvatore. "What are we doing here?"

He stroked her hand and drew a strand of hair away from her eyes. "This, my dear, is hopefully the church we'll be married in."

Maria's skin tingled. "Are you joking? Do not joke like that, for I'm not in the mood, Salvatore."

He threw his head back and laughed. "My darling Maria. I told you I would make all your dreams come true—and this is one of them."

She clasped her hands together. "Are you serious? We can get married—here?"

He nodded. "Only the best for you, my darling. Only the best."

She threw herself at him, embracing him tightly. Her mind was filled with ideas, preparations for the wedding, and joy. When they broke apart, they entered the church.

As she walked around the church, Maria grew more and more awed by its spaciousness and decor. There were paintings, mosaic decorations, a statue of Madonna with Child, and a central part of the church with two aisles on either side. An altar surrounded by stands featuring candles, colourfully potted flowers, and gold-encrusted walls and columns was too beautiful for words.

She couldn't believe she was getting married in this cathedral. It was her dream come true. True religious spirit was encapsulated in this church, and she'd be a part of that. She'd be a part of the cathedral's history, a part of all these centuries.

The priest, an older man with smiling eyes, arrived at the altar and introduced himself to Salvatore and Maria.

"Your husband-to-be, contacted me about your interest in this church. When is the special day?"

Maria looked to Salvatore. "We hadn't discussed a date yet, but soon."

Salvatore made a gesture with his hands. "I'd say within the next month. What do you say, Maria? Would that be okay with you?"

She pressed her hands together to keep them from shaking. She hadn't told the children yet. "Why not? A month from today?"

"Perfect." The priest smiled. "We were booked out until then, but we've had a recent cancellation."

Maria noticed a look pass between Salvatore and the priest. What was that about?

The priest added. "We do accept a small donation to the church on the day."

"Thank you, Father," Salvatore said. Maria nodded with a smile.

When the priest left, she lost her breath. They had actually booked this church for their wedding. It was time to tell her children. They had accepted Salvatore as a close family friend, so surely they'd accept him as a stepfather.

Chapter 17

DISCLOSURE

R oberto was sitting on the porch when his mother called him to come inside. Grey, stormy clouds came down, and with them, the smell of mist. He rose, entered the house, and watched as Edoardo and Angela put their school books away after doing homework.

Roberto hadn't been in the mood to do homework since his accident, and he knew he was failing miserably at school. Not that he cared much these days. Why should he, when he'd lost his ability to make things and use his craft? His wrist ached every time he tried to sand or cut a piece of wood. He couldn't make anything. It still hurt whenever he tried to lift something. He couldn't even do up his shirt buttons. He hoped it would heal eventually, as he felt helpless.

He squeezed onto the couch between his brother and sister, while his mother sat across from them on a chair with her hands clasped across her lap. Her face looked flushed, and she fidgeted and continually played with her hair. When she spoke, her voice shook.

"There—is something I need to tell you. Some—good news, I hope."

Roberto angled his head. "What is it?"

Edoardo smiled, but Angela frowned as if concerned. His mother took a deep breath, then resumed.

"Now, I know we've all been fortunate enough to have Salvatore as part of our family. He's helped us out so much, and we have a lot to thank him for."

"Yes, Mama. He seems to care a lot," Angela said.

"He has been coming here a lot lately too, Mama," Edoardo said.

Roberto was getting a sick feeling. His chest felt tight and his shoulders suddenly ached. Even his wrist was burning like hell. "Please tell us what's going on, Mama. Don't give us a speech, please."

His mother frowned. Then she swallowed and cleared her throat. "I care about Salvatore very much, and—well, how—how would you like it to be a permanent thing?"

Edoardo shifted. "What do you mean, Mama?"

She cleared her throat again. "Well—Salvatore and I are planning to get married."

Edoardo flung his arms around his mother, then Angela did the same. Roberto held back a heavy feeling in his stomach. A sudden coldness penetrated his body. He couldn't move and couldn't speak. This had to be a mistake. Surely he hadn't heard her right? She wasn't really planning to marry Salvatore, was she? It wasn't that long ago that his father had died. How could she move on so quickly? It was selfish of her. She was only thinking of herself.

What about their feelings? What about their need for more time? It was far too soon to be thinking of marrying someone else. Had she gone mad?

His mother got up from her seat and walked over to Roberto. She knelt in front of him and took his hand. "Are you okay with this, Roberto?"

He took a deep breath. "I don't know, Mama."

"He's a wonderful man and will take great care of us." She stroked his hand. "I only want the best for all of us."

Roberto looked away, fighting tears. No, he wouldn't cry in front of his mother. He had to be strong for her. She needed him now more than ever.

"Are you happy with Salvatore, Mama?"

She smiled. "Yes, he makes me very happy. He treats me with a lot of respect and he loves me."

"And—are you sure about this?" Roberto asked.

His mother nodded. "Yes, very sure." She paused. "He loves all of you, and only wants to make us happy."

"But, Papa?"

She blinked back tears. "Roberto, I will always love your father. That will never change just because I'm marrying another man. He will forever be in my heart."

"I miss Papa. I miss him a lot."

She leaned forward and gave him a tight hug. "I miss him too, darling." Then Edoardo and Angela joined in the embrace, and they huddled and cried together. Roberto felt the warmth in his body and smelled his mother's flowery perfume. While Angela hugged him hard enough to choke him, Edoardo patted him on the head. He loved his family.

Chapter 18

MATRIMONY

Maria's hands shook as she put on a long skirt and loose-fitting top, preparing for her wedding at the Duomo Salerno.

Salvatore had arranged a bus from the centre of Eboli for all the wedding guests. They were to be taken to the Duomo Salerno for the wedding ceremony, then to a local restaurant for the celebratory dinner. Maria was travelling in a private car arranged by Salvatore and planned to change into her wedding dress at the church.

She felt shivers down her spine. Numbness in her legs made her rest on the couch. She closed her eyes and took deep breaths, and when she opened them again, her gaze fell on a photo of Giovanni on the coffee table. Placing the photo against her heart, her mind cast her back to her own wedding to Giovanni. It was in the local Eboli Church where she walked down the aisle with a flutter in her heart when she spotted her husband to be. He had been a vision and had captured her heart completely.

Tears scalding her cheeks, she bowed her head and cried for her dear Giovanni. She missed him and would forever hold him close to her heart. Nothing and nobody could replace that.

She thought about the times they'd argued over money and realised how petty it was compared to the love they shared. If only she hadn't been hard on him. If only she'd accepted him for who he was and not put him under such immense pressure.

Maria prepared her bag, taking more deep breaths before she headed out. Her kindly neighbour and friend, Lucia, had offered to bring the children to the church while she prepared. Filippo had arrived from Germany the day before. With her wedding dress hanging under her arm and her bag in the other, she swung open the door and left.

Maria walked for a few minutes, then met with the driver who was taking her to the church. He was an old man with a scar across his cheek, but greeted her in an easy-going manner.

When she finally arrived, the magnetic beauty of the church took her breath away. A sense of exhilaration filled her as she proudly embarked on her new adventures with Salvatore. She was marrying a man who made her feel alive and invigorated. Hopefully, they'd be a family once her children adapted to their new lives.

Maria exited the car and thanked the driver. He bowed and she waved goodbye. Then she went into the changing room, where her neighbour and friend, Lucia sat, waiting.

"Well—about time you got here, woman. How long does it take for that driver of yours to bring you here?"

She approached and hugged her friend. "Thanks for helping out. Where are the children?"

Lucia stood and started unpacking the wedding dress from the suit bag.

"Oh, they're outside on the other side of the church, playing."

Maria touched her on the shoulder. "Thanks for having the children. It means a lot."

Lucia folded the wedding dress over one arm and held up the train with the other. She shook her head. "No need to thank me, woman. You deserve it. Now, let's get this dress on and make you look more beautiful than the principessa."

Maria's dress was made of tulle and organza, with a train that flowed outwards. It had a tight-fitted, long-sleeved bodice decorated with sequins and overlapping lace. A long veil reached the lower part of her back. Matching silk gloves complemented the look.

Once she finished dressing, she looked in the mirror and added the finishing touches of makeup. The green in her eyes lit up, and the blonde highlights glowed in her long, copper hair. The lipstick brought out the fullness of her lips, and the makeup enhanced her olive complexion. She almost looked exotic, and was very pleased with her appearance. She felt like a princess about to move in with her Prince Charming.

Lucia pulled her by the hand. "It's time."

Maria bit her lip, feeling tingling sensations in her fingers and toes, as well as butterflies in her stomach. She smoothed her dress and exhaled, closing her eyes momentarily. Then she left the room and found her father waiting outside the church.

She nodded to some of the guests who were yet to enter the church then joined her father. "I didn't know you were coming."

He tilted his head towards her. "Salvatore invited me. Thought we could start fresh. I hope you don't mind."

She sighed. "Well, it's something I didn't expect."

"Salvatore wanted to surprise you." He looked straight into her eyes. "I'm glad you're marrying someone who can take care of you." He gave her a kiss on both cheeks, then he took her arm and tucked it under his.

Maria didn't wish to argue. Besides, a part of her felt soothed by his presence. Maybe they could learn to sort out their differences. They followed the sound of the music and strolled down the aisle.

When she reached Salvatore, he leaned in and gave her a kiss. "So beautiful," he said.

Maria noticed a few women in the church shaking their heads. Yet, she didn't care what those women thought. She felt an overwhelming love for this man, and wondered why she'd never felt it before. Before Giovanni, she'd lusted after Salvatore, but her true love for Giovanni had overshadowed that lust. Now that Giovanni was gone, she felt that he'd want her to be happy without him. She knew that even though he and Salvatore never got along, he would be at peace knowing she was happy and that his family would be protected and taken care of.

The priest commenced the ceremony and joined them both in matrimony after they repeated their vows. When they finally kissed, claps and whistles filled the church. Then they broke apart, joined hands, and signed the papers at the altar. The soothing sounds of 'Ave Maria' played. Maria's knees felt weak as she signed the papers to seal their union.

As they strolled down the aisle and out the front door of the church, confetti and sugared almonds were thrown over them. They were greeted by family and friends. Maria found Filippo, Angela, and Edoardo, who all kissed and hugged her tightly while Roberto stood at a distance, his expression serious. When she hugged him, she sensed a tightness in his body.

"Are you okay, darling?"

He nodded. "Fine, Mama. You look really beautiful."

"Thanks, darling." She stroked his cheek.

Salvatore suddenly pulled her away. "We need to get some photos before the dinner, Maria. Come on, let's go."

She nodded and smiled reassuringly at Roberto who stood with his arms crossed and his lips pursed. Abruptly, he turned away and joined Andrea and his siblings.

Lucia left with the children and the other guests on the bus, heading to the local restaurant. They all attended the celebratory dinner in honour of the bride and groom. When it was over, Lucia took Maria and said, "You go on. I'll take care of the children."

Maria nodded, then left with Salvatore. Their driver took them to a hotel for the night. As they stepped into the hotel foyer, she gasped at the array of paintings of Italy's landscapes and farming villages. Sturdy white leather wooden benches and settees were arranged in a circular pattern with soft, blue cushions placed on each of them. A round glass table featured a glass vase with white orchids spilling out.

Salvatore completed a form and arranged for the room key. Then he turned to her and tapped her on the bottom. He gave her a cheeky grin as they entered the elevators and headed up to their room. Maria's hands were sweating, and the silence between them was unnerving. Even Salvatore was unusually quiet, and she knew why.

They took a tour of the rooms that were spacious with a small kitchenette, an open living area, mahogany furniture, a small television, a tan leather couch, and a laundry. In the bedroom there was a cast iron bed and a large curtained window as well as a tallboy and an armoire.

Maria took her veil off and started to unpack her bag, but Salvatore stopped her. He stroked her hand and kissed the side of her neck. She moaned in excitement. Slowly, he began undoing the buttons at the back of her dress. He pulled it off. Maria took off her petticoat but hesitated taking off her undergarments.

Salvatore said, "Let me take those off."

She allowed him to take control as he took off her bra and panties. He gazed at her as if burning right into her heart. Her breath and heart quickened as she stood there, naked, feeling exposed. When Salvatore took off his clothes, he lay her on the bed and kissed her hard on the mouth. His hands travelled over her breasts, circling her nipples until they were erect. She moaned, feeling hyper-aroused and kissed his neck and chest. She enjoyed hearing his soft moans. His hands explored every part of her body, and she felt alive and responsive to his every touch.

"Oh, Salvatore," she said.

"You are so sweet to touch," Salvatore said. "Let me love you, Maria."

Maria drew her hands into his hair as they kissed lingeringly. His hands slid down the sides of her breasts and hips. Then gently, he entered her. They climaxed at the same time. Then he put his arm around her, and they fell asleep in each other's arms.

Chapter 19

THE NEW JOURNEY

A few days later Filippo headed back to Germany and Salvatore and Andrea moved in with Roberto, Edoardo, Angela, and their mother. Roberto didn't mind living with Andrea. He was excited to see his best friend every day, but he wasn't sure about the new marriage yet. He hoped he'd get used to their new life.

Salvatore had got his housekeeper, Rosa another job in another part of the village and Roberto would miss her.

Andrea was taking Filippo's space so he'd share with Edoardo and Roberto, and Angela had her own bedroom.

His wrist was feeling much better, and he'd gone back to work in the barn outside the house. Salvatore had bought him the supplies and tools he needed, but he was still unable to complete a full piece of woodwork. As he started sanding his wrist would hurt. His left wrist was beginning to hurt too, but Salvatore encouraged him to not give up.

As they sat down for a dinner of fish fillet and roasted potatoes, Roberto's saliva worked overtime. This was a feast, as they'd never been able to afford this type of food. His fork pressed into the juices of the fish, the freshest fish he'd ever tasted, and the smell of spices and onions whetted his appetite. He cut his tender fish, and savoured the salty, flavoursome taste in his mouth. Juices dripped down his chin, and he wiped them away with a napkin, then took a sip of water. It was heaven to be eating like this. It was a change, and one he thought he could get used to. Roberto dug into his roast potatoes then addressed everyone at the table. "I was thinking I could go around to some of the houses further out to talk about my woodwork. What do you think, Salvatore?"

"Sounds like a good plan, but you'll need some business cards."

While Roberto was sipping his water, he saw Salvatore's trembling hand grab a glass filled with whisky.

"Do you think you could print them for me?"

Salvatore refilled his glass by pouring more whisky into it. "Sure. I have a printer friend of mine who could do it for you. Just write down what you want to say, and I'll get them done."

Roberto watched him drink. "Thanks."

He lifted his head up to watch his mother with an arm on Salvatore's shoulder.

"Darling, take it easy with the whisky. You're liable to get drunk."

Salvatore's jaw tightened. "Don't you worry, darling. I'm totally in control of my drinking."

Roberto turned to Andrea. His friend's head was bowed as he stared at his empty plate. Roberto kicked him under the table, but Andrea frowned and shook his head.

"What's with you?" Roberto whispered to Andrea.

"Nothing," Andrea said quickly. "Just eat."

Roberto looked over at Salvatore, who poured the remainder of the whisky into his glass. The bottle was empty.

When they finally finished eating, Angela and their mother cleared the table and did the washing up while Salvatore sat on the couch, smoking a cigar. The others huddled around the coffee table, playing cards. After an especially lucky round, Andrea jumped in excitement and accidentally spilled his orange juice onto the rug. He paled, quickly grabbed a wet tea towel and wiped the rug hard.

Salvatore rose and laid a hand on Andrea's shoulder. "Come with me."

He pushed Andrea into the bedroom.

Roberto gestured to his siblings to continue the game, then followed Salvatore and Andrea, his stomach sinking. Through a crack in the door, Roberto heard father and son talking.

Salvatore said, "How many times have I told you not to carry juice over to the living room? Just when we need to take care of and respect Maria's house."

"I'm sorry, Papa. It was an accident."

"But I've told you this before, and you continue to disobey me. What is wrong with you?"

Roberto held his breath and continued to listen.

"I won't do it again, Papa." Silence.

"We are part of a new family now so you need to step it up and be a man. No more acting like a little boy, you hear me?"

"But Papa—"

Roberto waited for a response but all he heard was a slap then another slap, followed by crying and finally, a banging sound. What was that? He could barely breathe, worried about the bang. Roberto's hand was on the door when he heard footsteps. Quickly, he made his way back to the living room, and squeezed in with his siblings. He tried to catch his breath.

"Are you okay?" Edoardo asked.

Before Roberto could respond, Salvatore returned and sat on the couch. He looked over at Roberto, and said, "You look like you've seen a ghost. What's wrong?"

Roberto shook his head. "Nothing. Just watching them play cards."

A few minutes later, Roberto excused himself. "I'm going to the bathroom," he said. As he walked back to his bedroom, he heard sobbing behind the door. He pushed the door open and saw Andrea wipe his eyes with the back of his hand.

Andrea sniffed and managed a forced smile. "What are you doing here?"

"Are you alright? I know what your Papa did."

Andrea tried to chuckle, but it sounded more like a sob. "What makes you think he did anything?"

"I was standing outside your door. I heard him slap you, then I heard a bang. What did he do to you?" Andrea lowered his head. He said nothing, but Roberto didn't give up. "Please tell me. I know he hit you, and he's done it before. Just tell me what else he did."

When he lifted his head up, Andrea's expression was solemn. "I deserved it, you know. I should listen to him more and I don't."

"That's no excuse for him to slap you. What was that bang I heard before?"

Andrea looked into the distance, and at that moment, Roberto noticed the gash across his elbow. Blood seeped out of it.

"What did he do Andrea? I'm not leaving here till you tell me."

After a few moments of silence, he said, "He pushed my elbow into the wall. It hurt like hell." He cleared his throat. "Please—do not tell anyone. Your Mama and my Papa just got married. Don't spoil anything."

Roberto knew Andrea was right. Their parents had only just got married, so why spoil it?

Roberto said, "For now, I won't say anything, but I'm keeping an eye on him."

Andrea nodded, his eyes darkening further. There was nothing more to say.

Chapter 20

ACCIDENT

"We are going bird hunting," Salvatore said. "It is the season."

Both Roberto and Andrea were at the bakery, helping him out on a Saturday. Salvatore usually didn't work on the weekends, but one of his workers was sick.

Roberto was washing bowls while Andrea dried them. The bits of dough stuck to the bowls as he scrubbed hard with the rough cloth. His fingernails chipped.

Salvatore peered into the oven to check on the bread. He wandered over to the boys and placed a hand on Roberto's shoulder. "We should be going."

"But I don't know how to use a gun," Roberto said.

"It's easy once you get the hang of it," said Andrea.

Salvatore wiped his hands on the apron he wore, then sat down. "I'll teach you, and I've cleared it with your mother, Roberto, so don't worry."

Roberto felt sick inside. He knew that killing animals was how families survived, but he'd never been hunting.

"Are you sure Mama is fine with this?"

"Perfectly. She understands that I have the experience." He smiled. "It is a common sport after all, and a necessity for food. It will be fun." He moved over to the oven and turned it off. Then he rushed into another room to prod one of his workers, who followed him back into the kitchen area. She was a short, chubby woman older than his mother, staring up at Salvatore with a grin. He seemed not to notice her expression as he pointed to the oven. She opened it, took the bread out of the oven and laid it gently on the counter.

Salvatore turned his attention back to them. "Besides, God made animals for us to survive. Now, let's go. We have no time to waste."

Andrea and Roberto finished with the bowls. Then Salvatore pulled them away. They headed to his car, and as he climbed into the back, Roberto smelled the stench of cigarettes and aftershave. He opened the window, the car feeling stuffy.

He bowed his head, closing his eyes, and wondered how he'd kill those tiny, innocent birds. His chest tightened, and the rest of his body tensed up as he looked out the window. The landscape blurred as the car shot past.

Roberto rubbed the back of his neck, an empty feeling in the pit of his stomach. His mouth was dry, and his head felt like it might explode. Why did he have to do this? He wasn't ready to hunt, and probably never would be. Wasn't that a sport for fathers who had to provide for their families?

Passing through a deserted road, Roberto saw an old woman carrying a vase of water on top of her head. Then he peered at a man and a young boy pushing a donkey along a winding path, the man wiping the brow of the younger boy, who was sweating. It reminded Roberto of the days he'd worked with his father, and how proud he was spending time bonding and helping his father in time of need.

By the time Salvatore pulled over, it had been a long time since they'd seen anyone. They parked at the end of a long, winding path in a deserted area surrounded by rocks. Salvatore got out of the car. He approached the rocks and sat while his eyes searched the surrounds. Then he turned back towards the car and gestured for the boys to get out. Watching Salvatore retrieve three rifles from the boot of the car, Roberto's heart skipped a beat. They looked huge. He'd never even handled a rifle, so how did Salvatore expect him to shoot one now? Was this man insane to think he wanted to personally kill pigeons? He didn't want to complain to his mother. She was happy in her new marriage, and he wanted to keep it that way. Salvatore doted on her, and they seemed to love each other a lot. He was pleased that his mother had found someone she could live with.

Before Salvatore picked up the rifle, he took a little sip from his flask. He wiped his mouth with the back of his hand, closing his eyes as if continuing to taste the drink.

Roberto stood, his feet unsteady as his stepfather presented the rifle. Salvatore pointed to and named the different parts of the gun and showed Roberto where to pull the trigger. He tapped his fingers on the stock looking far into the distance, then handed Roberto the rifle. He tried to steady the rifle against his shoulder. It felt heavy, like lead. His shoulder hurt, and he just wanted to go home.

Salvatore pointed to a nearby tree trunk and said, "Aim at that tree. That's the way. Hold it like that. Now pull the trigger." Roberto hesitated, wondering what it would feel like to actually fire a gun. "Come on, you need to practice into that trunk. Shoot!"

Roberto pulled the trigger and recoiled. The rifle stock jammed hard into his shoulder and he fell backward as if he'd been punched in the chest. The bullet hit the tree with a loud crack. It was a deafening, chilling sound.

Salvatore smiled. "Good. You'll get the hang of it."

The wind was picking up, leaves falling gently from the trees and swirling to the ground. Roberto liked the stillness of the woods, a quiet broken only by the flutter of leaves. He couldn't see anyone else in the distance, and he liked that too.

Suddenly, a flock of birds rose from the underbrush. Salvatore got his rifle ready and aimed at the flock of pigeons, shooting three times. His aim was good, as three of the birds fell from the sky like steaming raindrops.

Salvatore grinned and turned towards his son. "Now, it's your turn, Andrea. Make it quick. There aren't many others coming."

Andrea picked up his rifle from the ground, heaved with the intense weight, aimed, then pulled the trigger. The shot echoed as his body recoiled slightly. Andrea pulled the trigger again. As the sound penetrated the area, a pigeon fell. Andrea smiled and put the rifle down. "Yes! I finally got one."

Roberto sighed. Salvatore turned to him and gave him the sign to shoot. He placed the rifle against his right shoulder and aimed towards the sky. This time, he closed his eyes. The pain of death was unbearable to watch. He didn't want to be killing birds but he could feel Salvatore's presence behind him, so he braced himself for the recoil and pulled the trigger. When the crack of the rifle had faded, he opened his eyes. He had missed.

"Keep going," Salvatore said. "You're doing this until you get one down. Don't stop."

Roberto's stomach sank, his breathing becoming shallower. His shoulder hurt, but he aimed the rifle again. He missed again, and Salvatore pointed to the rifle. "Let's do it!"

He was third time lucky when a pigeon plunged from the sky, but Roberto felt numb.

When Salvatore patted him on the back, Roberto managed a smile. "You did it, my boy. You killed one."

Salvatore put down his rifle, reached into his coat pocket, and took another few sips of his flask. When he walked, he was wobbly on his feet. He squinted in the bright sun and took more sips from his flask. He turned to Roberto. "How about you go get the sacks for the birds," he said. His words slurred.

Roberto jogged towards the sacks, appreciating the warmth of sunlight on his skin. He wondered where Andrea had gone. He looked around but couldn't find him. He opened the car door and grabbed a few sacks, then began circling outward, getting further from where they'd hunted. "Andrea, where are you? Andrea?"

An uneasy feeling settled deep in his stomach. His legs weighed heavily as he trudged back to the hunting ground where Salvatore was. Two sudden shots made him jump. Hadn't Salvatore stopped shooting? Or was it Andrea shooting?

He held on to the sacks and headed towards Salvatore, who was holding the rifle in shaking hands. He reached for the flask again and took another sip. Roberto didn't like what he was seeing.

"Where are the pigeons?" Roberto asked.

"Right by that tree. Give me those sacks." They walked for a few minutes until they reached the dead birds. Salvatore roughly threw them into the sacks and asked, "Where's Andrea?"

Roberto shrugged. "I don't know. He must've wandered off."

Salvatore stormed over to a larger, towering tree. "I found another beauty and couldn't let it get away."

Roberto shook his head. "I thought you'd stopped shooting. Don't you have enough?"

"It's a sport. It's never enough."

Stepping into loose, dry branches and fighting the glaring sun, Roberto followed his stepfather towards the tree and cringed when he saw the bird. It was still fluttering around. Roberto wanted to save it, but it was too late.

Salvatore picked it up and broke its neck. Roberto gasped. He swallowed and turned away, feeling a pain in his stomach. His heart broke in two for that tiny bird. Why couldn't they save it?

Salvatore watched Roberto. "Sorry you had to see that, but he would've suffered. He would've died eventually."

Roberto nodded. "I've never seen anything like that."

Salvatore ignored the comment. "Let's find Andrea."

They called out to him, but there was no response. They walked around the path and between trees but it was deserted, not another soul in sight. The sun was going down so fairly soon they'd need to get home, but they had to find Andrea first.

"Andrea, where are you? Andrea," said Salvatore.

As he walked around the area, Roberto's heart raced. His body felt cold. Why did he have a horrible feeling? Why were his hands trembling? It must've been the mild breeze, that was all.

As he crunched over twigs, rocks, and leaves, he saw something that froze him in his spot. It was Andrea's shoe jutting from a pile of brush. His stomach felt heavy. He couldn't move. He wasn't even sure if he was breathing.

"What's wrong?" He heard Salvatore as if from a distant place. "Roberto, what is it?"

He managed to point. "Andrea—over there."

Salvatore turned, stumbled towards his son, shaking like a man immersed in ice. "Andrea—no. No!" He rushed over to Andrea's crumpled body and bent to feel for a pulse. Andrea lay still, frozen and motionless. He looked dead.

Chapter 21

REALITY CHECK

S alvatore put his hand over Andrea's heart. "He's breathing, thank God, but it's slow." His face flushed as he wiped his brow. "We can't move him."

Roberto was shaking. "Why not?"

"We could do more damage. You wait here—I'll go get help. Do not take your eyes off him for one second." Salvatore jumped up and ran for the car.

Roberto held his friend's hand, listening to Andrea's shallow breathing. "Please hang on, Andrea. Your father's gone to get help." He closed his eyes, hoping it was all a bad dream. "You're going to be okay. You're going to be okay. Please hang on."

He saw blood everywhere, all around Andrea's back. When he touched his friend, his hand came away covered in blood. Andrea's lifeless look made Roberto want to die. He just wanted his best friend to wake up.

He wasn't sure how long he waited near that tree. It seemed like hours, but he kept checking his friend's breathing and pulse every few minutes. He held on to Andrea's hand, looking at his pale face. If only he would stir or make some conscious sound, but he didn't. Roberto prayed to God that Andrea would make it to the hospital. He didn't want Andrea to die like his Papa because the doctor was too late with the medication. It couldn't happen again. He wouldn't let it.

His body ached from sitting for so long. His feet were numb, his mouth dry, his eyes sore. His face felt cold in the wind but he continued to stroke Andrea's hand as if it could breathe life into him. Again, he checked Andrea's pulse, and was relieved to feel a thready heartbeat. Where was Salvatore? Why did it have to take so long?

Suddenly, he heard the sound of an engine. He looked up to see Salvatore's car bouncing down the path with its headlights on, the ambulance behind him. He was thankful that Salvatore had status and wealth in the community, and was able to get an ambulance here this soon. Roberto breathed a sigh of relief.

Salvatore burst out of the car and rushed to Andrea's side. "How is he?"

"Not good," Roberto said. "But still breathing."

"I came as fast as I could" Salvatore knelt beside his son. "I couldn't find a working phone and had to drive all the way to the hospital." A man and a woman climbed out of the ambulance and hurried over with a stretcher. The man was bulky, the woman tall.

"Oh, this looks really bad," said the woman.

The man gave the woman a concerned look. "We'll check him out and get him stable," he said. "We'll do everything we can for him, don't worry."

The woman helped the man as they checked Andrea's wound and put some kind of mask over his face. Then they gently placed him onto the stretcher and wheeled him into the ambulance.

Salvatore touched Roberto on the shoulder. "Let's go to the hospital."

Roberto nodded and followed Salvatore into the car.

Salvatore followed the ambulance in silence, hands white-knuckled on the steering wheel. The ride to the hospital seemed to take forever, and Roberto spent it in mute and desperate prayer. When they finally reached the Salerno Hospital, the attendants wasted no time with Andrea. They whisked him straight inside, leaving Roberto and Salvatore to follow numbly behind them.

Roberto's body felt heavy, and a sickening feeling came over him as he walked into emergency.

"Don't worry we'll take care of him," said the man as they took Andrea away. Roberto sat in a quiet corner of the waiting area and Salvatore sank into a seat beside him, gazing silently into the distance. It was like he wasn't even there.

Salvatore and Roberto sat in silence with their heads bowed. They waited for a long time, watching a stream of exhausted-looking people in bandages being shuffled in and out of the waiting room. Then the doctor, a bearded man with deep blue eyes. walked to them. "Are you Andrea's father, Mr Adessi?"

Salvatore rose and shook his hand. "Yes, doctor. How is he?"

"We removed the bullet but it penetrated and tore into his mid-to lower back. The good news is, the spinal cord wasn't severed, but there's a lot of trauma to that area."

Roberto looked away, heartbroken.

"What does that mean, doctor?" Salvatore asked.

"In some cases, victims of gunshot wounds recover most of their function within the first six months but in other cases, the paralysis and loss of function below the spine can be permanent."

Roberto wanted to scream but he kept his hand pressed against his mouth. He turned away for a moment. His legs felt like jelly. He wished he could lie down.

Salvatore pressed hard against his cheeks. "So you're saying he may never walk again?"

"Yes, but with physical therapy and medication to manage the pain, he may recover."

Salvatore swallowed. He grabbed the doctor's arm tightly. "What else, doctor?"

"Well, I don't want to speculate, but there could be loss of bladder and bowel function. Also, nerve pain, unstable blood pressure and blood flow. It is too soon to tell though, and he'll need to stay in the hospital for a while to make sure he remains stable."

Salvatore swallowed hard and said faintly, "Thank you, doctor."

The doctor nodded and left. Salvatore sank into the seat, covered his face with his hands, and cried. Roberto touched his shoulder, but Salvatore shrugged it away. Roberto felt hurt by the gesture, but he understood some of the pain his stepfather was in.

As he followed Salvatore from the hospital, Robert's legs wobbled and his head felt light. It felt like he was breathing through wet cloth. Wordlessly, Salvatore flung open the passenger door then stalked around to the driver's side. They drove home as they'd driven to Salerno. In silence.

Chapter 22

PUTTING BACK THE PIECES

When Roberto and Salvatore finally reached the house some time later, Angela was cutting carrots while Edoardo and Filippo were putting wood in the fireplace. Their mother was stirring soup on the stove. The family turned in greeting, but Roberto's insides felt all muddled. He wanted to crawl under a rock and never come out. Salvatore walked as if his legs couldn't carry him. He headed towards Mama and grabbed her hand. Roberto hung back.

"Where did you go? We thought you'd left us, or something," Mama said.

Edoardo joked. "Yeah, I think I was about to steal your bed. Thought you were dead or something," He was always the joker, Roberto thought. Always looking at the bright side of life.

"I know you went bird hunting, but all this time?"

Angela angled her head, frowning. "So where are the birds? Thought we'd have them for dinner."

Salvatore swallowed, his head bowed. Tears streamed down his face.

"I—I have to—"

Mama frowned. "And where's Andrea? He must be hungry by now."

Nobody answered her, but Edoardo intervened. "You're the lucky one, Roberto. You go to have a hunt, and we get stuck here doing chores. That's hardly fair. You must be Salvatore's favourite."

His mother stared Salvatore straight in the eyes and stroked his face. "My darling, what happened? You both look like you've seen a ghost. And where's Andrea? Please tell us. You're scaring me."

Salvatore sat down, rubbing his flushed cheeks. "Andrea—he's in the hospital." He drew a quivering hand through his damp hair, then rubbed his eyebrow. "I need to get back."

Angela set down the knife and came to huddle around Salvatore with Edoardo and their mother. "What happened?"

Roberto stepped into the kitchen, and Angela slid closer to Edoardo to make room in the circle. Roberto said, "It was an accident, but hopefully he'll be okay." He blinked back his tears. "He just walked off and we couldn't find him. Then—"

"It was all my fault," Salvatore said to Mama. "I didn't see him— in the distance. I shot him when—I didn't see him." He clutched the shirt above his heart and looked at the ground, stricken. "All my fault. It's all my fault."

Mama hugged Salvatore tightly, crying softly. She turned to Roberto and did the same. They huddled together as a family, a moment of silence.

Roberto's mother tugged Salvatore towards the couch and said, "We'll get a hotel in Salerno so we can be close by. I'll organise it with Lucia to care for the kids for a while. Whatever you need."

Salvatore nodded, and again they hugged. Roberto wondered if things would ever be the same. How would their lives change with Andrea in a wheelchair, unable to dress himself or go to the toilet without help? What would it be like not to walk again or not go to the toilet on your own? He swallowed past the lump in his throat and prayed Andrea would be okay.

Chapter 23

PERSONAL CHANGES

It was a month before Andrea was well enough to come home. He'd had his surgery and rehabilitation in the hospital, but was still recovering.

Roberto, Edoardo, Angela, and Lucia waited anxiously in the living room trying to play cards, and taking turns going to the window to look for the car. When they heard the sound of the car doors slamming, they scurried to the car and waited beside it, huddling together as if for courage. They watched with anxious eyes for Andrea's appearance.

Salvatore grabbed the wheelchair from the boot and unfolded it. He then wheeled it to the back car door, gently picked Andrea up, and eased him into the wheelchair.

Andrea didn't respond. He slouched in the chair, his face lifeless and his eyes dead. Their mother wheeled Andrea inside while Salvatore walked unsteadily behind them, frowning. As he passed, he gave the children a silent nod and rubbed his bloodshot eyes.

Andrea stared at the children and Lucia but said nothing. He bowed his head, his expression dark and flat.

Salvatore hadn't shaved. His chin was covered in stubble, and deep dark circles bruised the skin under his eyes. He appeared to have shrunk in height and his usual strong posture and eye contact were gone. Roberto's mother, on the other hand, looked a bit more hopeful as she hugged all her children and Lucia. She beamed and took a deep breath as if thankful to be finally home. Grabbing Lucia's hand, she said, "Thank you for having the children. I do appreciate it."

Salvatore turned away without acknowledging Lucia. He left for the kitchen and poured a glass of water, then sat on his own at the kitchen table. His hands shook as he brought the glass to his lips. His eyes peered into the distance. Andrea watched him, then looked down into his lap without speaking.

Lucia ignored the silent exchange between Salvatore and Andrea. She turned to Mama. "Any time darling. I'll just get you to return the favour when I have my own little ones. Hopefully just like yours."

Lucia was married, but being younger than his mother, didn't have her own children yet. She'd make a great mother one day, thought Roberto.

"Of course," Mama whispered in Lucia's ear, but Roberto heard. "So did your husband put bars in the bathroom?"

"Sure did, darl. Don't you worry. Just let me know if there's anything else you need."

She waved away Mama's thanks, then kissed everyone and said goodbye to Salvatore, who grunted in response. Pretending not to notice his sour mood, Lucia turned to the rest of the family. "See you soon. Bye."

When Lucia had gone, Mama and Angela started preparing dinner while Andrea wheeled himself into the bedroom. Roberto and Edoardo sat on the couch, not knowing what to say to one another. Finally, Roberto sighed, retreated into the kitchen and turned to his stepfather.

"How is he?" Roberto asked.

Salvatore flinched. "How do you think he is? Peachy?"

Roberto drew back and shrugged. "I know it's hard for him. How can I help?"

Salvatore sighed and shook his head. "You know, if you had looked out for him, then maybe none of this would have happened."

Tears sprang to Roberto's eyes, and the hair lifted on the back of his neck. Abruptly, Salvatore rose and slammed his chair hard against the table. While the family sat in shocked silence, he stormed outside, leaving the door open. Roberto felt a quiver in his stomach, then he rose to close the door. He watched as Salvatore strode off into the distance with his hands in his pockets.

Roberto returned to the kitchen. For the first time, he noticed his mother had lost weight too. She was cutting zucchini into cubes then dropping them into a pot of boiling water. Turning to him, she said, "You know it's not your fault?" She gave him a quick hug, then returned to stirring the soup. "It's hard for him, darling. He's not thinking straight. Just be patient and give him time to get used to the situation. I'm sure he'll come around soon."

Roberto nodded, a numbness spreading through his whole body. "But Andrea—he's finding it hard too, isn't he?"

His mother nodded. "Yes, because now we have to help him with everything. He can't walk so he needs help getting into bed, going to the toilet, and having a shower.

Even getting dressed is hard for him." She wiped her brow with a tissue. "We need to be patient, Roberto."

He nodded. "Do you think I can go talk to Andrea?"

"Sure, darling, but don't pressure him to talk if he's not ready to, okay?"

"Okay, Mama."

Roberto cleared his throat and was about to go and see his friend when Andrea called out for their mother. She dropped the soup spoon onto the counter and headed to the bedroom. Roberto trailed behind her. He watched outside the door as Andrea whispered something to Mama, who slid one arm beneath Andrea's thighs and the other around his trunk, and carried him to the toilet, kicking the door closed behind them. Roberto cringed, thinking how hard it must be for Andrea to have to expose himself like that.

He wondered what his mother had to do to help Andrea. How much could his friend do for himself now?

When Andrea was carried back to his room, his body was floppy and he hung over his mother's shoulder, completely unfocused. His face was a blank mask.

Some time later Salvatore arrived, but his mood hadn't changed. His teeth were clenched, and so were his fists, but he didn't speak. Neither did the rest of them. They sat down to dinner, preparing to eat a bowl filled with vegetable soup and garlic bread. His mother pushed Andrea in his wheelchair, but his body stiffened and he didn't look at anyone.

Edoardo, the joker said, "So did you see any pretty nurses at the hospital, Andrea?"

Andrea shrugged and looked at his father, who frowned as Edoardo went on. "Come on. Tell me what it was like at the hospital. Did you get ice-cream?"

Andrea averted his eyes. "Yes, I did."

"Did they treat you well? The nurses, I mean?" Edoardo asked.

Andrea nodded dully. "I—I—guess they treated me well."

"Good." Angela smiled. "Because we missed you around here."

Mama said to Angela "And I heard that you were all well behaved while we were gone."

"Yes, Mama," Angela said. "We did all that Lucia told us to do."

They were chattering about school and their homework when Salvatore interrupted. "You all need to help out around here. Things are going to be different, so I want Roberto to do more of the housework and Angela to do all of the cooking. Edoardo, you can help me in the bakery, and Andrea—."

"Only if I get to see pretty girls," Edoardo interrupted.

Salvatore slammed his fist hard on the table, shocking everyone. Roberto jumped and his mother gasped. Edoardo stared into his soup, silent. Only Andrea showed no reaction.

Through gritted teeth, Salvatore said, "Always making a stupid joke. Well this is real life now so adapt to it." He turned back to Andrea. "Andrea, you'll have to catch up on all your schoolwork."

Andrea's back stiffened. "I know, Papa. I will."

His mother looked pained. "But Salvatore, we haven't even discussed this. Don't you think—"

He held his hand up. "I don't want to hear it. I've made my decision, and that's final." He turned away, tore the bread into tiny shreds, then shoved some into his mouth and chewed it thoroughly.

The darkness in his mother's eyes broke Roberto's heart. She cleared her throat and focused her energy on the soup, not meeting her husband's gaze.

The energy in the kitchen was quiet and tense. Roberto put his hand on Andrea's shoulder. Without meeting his gaze, Andrea pulled his shoulder away. Roberto wondered if Salvatore would ever get over this issue with his son, or whether Salvatore's actions had doomed their relationship for life? He hoped not, for all their sakes.

Chapter 24

ABUSE

A week later, towards the end of September, Maria, Salvatore, and the children planned to visit the Bay of Salerno to celebrate their patron saint, San Matteo. She remembered visiting the Bay of Salerno when she was five with her parents. This was the reason she was able to convince Salvatore to take her to the Amalfi Coast; to savour the memories she'd had with her mother. She explained that having an escape from the house was healthy for the family, as they needed the break. In the end, he was convinced.

As they stood by the front door, preparing to leave, Andrea held up his hand. "I don't want to go."

Maria angled her head. "But, dear, it'd be good for you to get out. Get some fresh air."

He shook his head. "I just feel tired."

Roberto stepped in. "I'll stay with him. You all go."

Edoardo and Angela looked at each other. "No, I'll stay," said Angela. She drew a hand through her hair and moved closer to Andrea.

"Angela, I'm happy to stay. You all go have fun. Not to worry." Maria looked over at Salvatore, who shuffled his feet and stared at the ground. A muscle in his cheek pulsed.

Andrea watched his father for a moment then turned to Roberto. "You're going Roberto. I'll get Lucia to stay with me."

Maria sighed. "Listen, Andrea. Lucia—you might not—"

Andrea frowned. "It's okay. I'll be fine with her."

Roberto knelt in front of his friend and touched him on the knees. "Don't you know that I can look after you? No need to get Lucia."

Maria sighed and watched the two friends as Andrea shook his head but remained silent. Roberto sighed, as if resigning himself to the situation, then moved over to the couch. As hard as it would be for Andrea to stay with Lucia, it was worse for him to go out. He wasn't ready to face the world just yet.

Taking a deep breath, she hurried out the door and hoped that Lucia was available. It'd be easier for her to come to the house, given that Andrea was comfortable here.

When she returned with Lucia, her friend turned to Andrea. "You know, dear, I've had lots of experience babysitting so we'll have lots of fun. We can play cards."

Andrea nodded, fidgeting while Lucia waved her arms up in the air to shoo them away. "Now all of you leave. Andrea and I will be just fine." She started pushing Andrea out the door so that they could watch the others leave. His brow was furrowed, and he continually shifted his posture as if he couldn't get comfortable.

When they finally got in the car, Maria breathed a sigh of relief. They all needed a change from the four walls. She hoped the children would enjoy the Amalfi coast as much as she did.

Though a had week passed since Salvatore's outburst, Maria couldn't help but be concerned for her new husband, whose moods seemed to be getting worse. She'd tried to reach him, but he'd been detached and reserved, refusing to talk about his feelings. She was certain that in time he would adapt to these changes.

They left in the car, and as Salvatore was driving she cringed as slowly the speed crept up over the speed limit. His eyes focused straight ahead, and after he'd driven for ten minutes, his mood soured even further when a driver in front slowed him down.

"Bastardo. Move or I'll make you move," Salvatore shouted. Maria's chest tightened, and she pressed a hand to her heart. He drove frighteningly close to the driver in front, who refused to drive faster. Salvatore also refused to budge. Instead, he stayed close to the vehicle, continuing to curse in a loud tone. "Move it, will you? I don't have all day."

Maria laid a hand on his arm. "He can't hear you, darling. Just relax. There's no hurry—we have plenty of time."

He shook his head. "I didn't even want to go to this stupid festival. Why did you make me come? Lucia could've taken you, for God's sake."

She drew back. "Salvatore, please. The children," she whispered.

He ignored her when the driver in front changed lanes. Salvatore breathed a sigh of relief, then sped all the way to Salerno.

Maria turned to see the children's cowered postures and complete focus on peering out their side windows. She realised they too were having a hard time with Andrea's disability, but at least they didn't lash out like her husband. He vented his feelings in the most negative way.

Maria looked out the window, gazing at the stretch of mountains and coastline. A small mist hovered in the background, but the scenery was still majestic and rich with colour. In the distance, tiny looking houses were stacked around the mountains, and situated at an angle to the sea below. Boats and fisherman caught their catch along the coast. It was breathtaking, and Maria needed to take her mind off their problems at least for the day.

When they reached the Bay of Salerno, she watched the swarms of people rushing around with their families, while others drove around in search of a car park. Salvatore huffed as he found a lot of spaces filled up. He shook his head, braked for a moment, then pulled at his shirt collar. He closed his eyes and pondered. Maria noticed he was trying to calm himself down. She kept her eyes peeled for any parking spaces.

When finally a driver pulled out of a space, Maria sighed with relief. "Here's a spot."

Salvatore opened his eyes and exhaled. "Finally. I was so close to leaving this place." He drove into the spot, parked, and they made their way out onto the street. Salvatore turned to her while Roberto, Edoardo, and Angela walked behind. "I cannot believe all of these people, just to honour a saint."

Maria ignored him and headed on through the small passageways in the centre of Salerno. As they reached the beginning of the procession in the street, she was pushed and prodded by the huge crowd. People stepped on her toes, young children shoved her, and she struggled to find Roberto, Edoardo, and Angela in the crowd until she called out to them. Salvatore moved on up ahead as if he couldn't get away from her fast enough.

Finally settling on a spot clear enough to see the procession, Maria put an arm around Roberto and another around Angela. Edoardo jumped up and down for a better view due to his small size, while Salvatore stood back, then returned closer to Maria's side. He nuzzled up close.

"I'm sorry about before." He kissed her on the cheek.

"It's okay." She beamed. "Let's have a good time today."

He nodded. "I love you, darling."

Her Salvatore was finally back. "And I love you too."

Maybe he was starting to realise that life with a disabled son was okay. It didn't have to be the end of their lives, but just a new way of doing things. She loved Andrea like her own child, and would never turn him away because of his disability. Salvatore knew that.

As the procession in the street started, Maria was in awe of the countless men dressed in colourful attire carrying the statue of the Protector and Patron saint of Salerno. Boxed-up candles surrounded the statue of the saint resting on a raised timber platform. Musicians and the Military paraded down the street, either playing music or marching. The crowds cheered them on, clapping, and shouted muffled words. Maria turned to see a young boy of about five in a wheelchair nodding his head in excitement. A man whom she assumed was his father huddled over and picked him up. He lifted the child, who had the widest smile she'd ever seen, onto his shoulders. What a beautiful little boy. He was in a wheelchair, yet he didn't let that deter him in life. He was loved and that was all that mattered. The boy clapped his hands and watched the parade. Maybe if Salvatore saw that, he would see sense.

The boy's legs were floppy over the man's shoulders and he shouted, "Papa.' He nodded while watching the show and the man lifted his hand up to stroke the boy's hair, but the boy shrugged him away. He probably didn't want to be distracted when he wanted to watch the show. The rapport between them was close though, and it was beautiful to watch the connection.

Maria turned to see the children watching, but when she turned to the other side, Salvatore was silently crying beside her. He was watching the little boy with a deep yearning, yet a sense of hopelessness, like he had greater hopes for this boy than he did for Andrea.

Salvatore rubbed his eyes and lifted his head up to watch the procession. Maria took a deep breath and felt a tightness in her chest. She continued to watch the parade, deciding to give Salvatore his space to grieve quietly.

After some time, she turned to point out a broken wheel on a carriage to Salvatore but he was no longer beside her. Maybe he went to the men's room. No doubt he'd be back soon. Maybe he just needed time to himself, to get his bearings and let his tears out. That was okay. She'd wait.

On the other side, Roberto was clapping, Angela was moving her head to the music, and Edoardo was dancing on the spot. She laughed at their focus on the festivities and felt warmed by their joy in the religious celebration. She and Giovanni had raised them well, and they all had beautiful souls. She was truly blessed.

Some time had passed, and Maria felt sick. Salvatore was still missing, and he'd been missing for a while now. She was beginning to worry and wondered where he might've gone.

She turned to Roberto and grabbed him gently by the shoulders. "Have you seen Salvatore?"

"No, Mama."

Edoardo overheard. "Oh, he'll be back. Don't worry."

"We can go find him, Mama," said Angela.

Maria nodded, then ushered the children out of the crowded area towards the passageways. Roaming the streets, she passed by shops that Salvatore may have entered and looked inside their windows. She spotted bars and restaurants, a ceramic crockery shop, a clothing store selling all the current designer fashions, and a store selling limoncello, which was a drink made from the local Amalfi lemons. Finally she noticed a bottle shop that sold local and international wines. Was he in there? She hoped not. She couldn't really enter some of these places with her children. She continued to wander but her husband was nowhere to be found.

"We need to find Salvatore," she said. "Where could he have gone?"

Roberto stopped her in her tracks. "It's like he just disappeared."

Angela knit her brows. "Are you okay, Mama? I'm sure we'll find him. He can't be too far."

"He's probably gone to the toilet," said Edoardo, pressing his hand against his mouth as if to suppress a laugh. "Mama, let me find him. Wait for me here. It will be quicker if I run around those shops over there."

Maria drew back. "No, Edoardo. We should stay together."

"I won't be long. Just wait for me."

With a trembling hand held to her chest, she closed her eyes.

"You know he's the fastest runner at school, Mama. He'll be quick."

The waiting was unbearable, but she had faith in her son. Faith that he would return, but he was still too young to be wandering a strange city on his own.

When Edoardo returned, he was out of breath and leaned over. "Sorry, Mama. Couldn't find him anywhere."

"Let's go together, and stay close," Maria said.

Maria's heart beat faster as each passageway she approached was empty. She willed herself not to panic. What was he thinking? To leave them alone in this crowded chaos? For the children's sake, she took a deep breath and tried to calm herself. "I'm sure we'll get a chance to go to the church for the ceremony. Then they'll have the fireworks later tonight."

"Sounds good," said Roberto.

Bile in her throat kept her frozen to the ground. Was he hurt? Did he just need time to himself? How would they get home if Salvatore went missing?

Maria finally saw him hunched up close to a towering tree in a deserted street. No wonder he'd come here. Nobody could see him here. Nobody could see what he was doing.

She cringed. Salvatore held a bottle of wine in his trembling hands, drinking from the bottle. It was almost finished. He wiped his mouth with the back of his hand then sat on the concrete ground, his head lowered. Was he still crying?

She turned to her children. "You please wait here. Do not move. I won't be long."

They all nodded, aware of who was up ahead.

Maria made her way to Salvatore. She bent down to the ground and tried lifting him up, but he shoved her away. "Leave me alone."

"Salvatore please. You have to stop this. The children can see you."

"I—don't care," he slurred. He stood up suddenly, swaying on his feet.

"Come on, please stop drinking. Andrea wouldn't want you to be like this. You need help. Please come with me."

His face hardened, his eyes squinting as he fisted his hands.

"Don't you bring Andrea into this. He should—should have been here, and now—now he's crippled because—because of me. All me." He turned away.

"Darling, Andrea's fine. He will get better, you'll see."

Salvatore shook his head. "You don't know that."

"I have faith, but for now you have to stop drinking. You cannot cope this way. Think of the children. Think of me." She touched him on the shoulder. "Andrea will be fine."

His eyes darkened and his face reddened. "You shut your damn mouth. Always trying to control me." He swung his right hand back and punched Maria hard across the mouth. She fell back, tasting copper, and hit her head on the ground. For a moment, she lay stunned. A trickle of warmth seeped from her mouth, and she covered it with her hand. Roberto, Angela and Edoardo quickly moved to her side.

Roberto reached her first. "Mama, are you okay? Mama."

Maria's head pounded and her mouth burned. She tried to push herself up, but a wave of dizziness washed over her. She sank back to the ground, too spent to rise.

She squinted at Salvatore. Her vision was blurred, so she could barely make out his features. He sank back into a crouch and kept drinking his wine, ignoring all of them. It was as if he were oblivious to the effects of his current actions on his family. He didn't even seem to care. Completely selfish, and yet he looked so broken.

Maria steeled her heart. She wondered how she could have found him attractive. How could she take him back? Yet, how would they cope without him?

Roberto moved into action and enlisted the help of a nearby couple. They came to Maria's aid, helping her up and offering to give them a ride to the hospital. The couple appeared to be in their twenties. The woman had curly red hair, friendly eyes, and a soft expression, while the man was robust with dark eyes and a crooked nose.

"No need for a hospital," Maria said. "I'll be fine. What we do need is a ride back home to Eboli."

"Of course, but what do we do about him?" The man asked, nodding towards Salvatore.

"Please, can you look after him?" She turned to the man. "He's drunk but I don't want him home. Just make sure he's taken care of." Maria handed the man some money but he refused.

The young woman put her arm around Maria. "I'll take care of you, don't worry. The car's not very far." She smiled at the children. "But don't you think we should take you to the hospital?"

Maria pressed a hand against her throbbing, aching head. "No, I'll be fine with rest. Thank you."

Salvatore crouched on the ground, crying while the man pulled him up. Maria had little sympathy for him, for he had crossed the line. Would he ever change his ways? Did he even want to?

Chapter 25

FORGIVENESS

M aria, Roberto, Edoardo, and Angela arrived home safely without Salvatore. She thanked the young woman as she stepped inside the house. Her feet felt heavy. A sick feeling settled in her stomach as she took some deep breaths, ignoring her pain.

She lowered herself on the bench, then realised the house was too quiet. Lucia must have taken Andrea to her house. "Children," she called. "Andrea is at Lucia's. We need to go and get him." As they hurried out the door, an emptiness swept over her. She hoped Salvatore was warm and safe, but for the sake of the children, she couldn't have him home until he'd sobered up.

Maria walked along the dirt path with her children, feeling the autumn wind brushing her face. The trees thrashed about as she struggled to walk the track. She was grateful for Roberto's arm around her. Her legs felt like lead, and she just wanted to sleep.

Before she could knock, the door swung open. Looking at Maria, Lucia's face went ashen. As they were ushered inside, Maria smelled warm bread and the aroma of spices and meatball sauce with a hint of parsley and basil. She was famished as they hadn't had a chance to eat dinner. Lucia invited them to stay, but remained quiet in front of the children. She was good that way, always knowing when to speak and when to stay silent.

Andrea was reading near the couch, completely focused on his book until Angela and Edoardo moved to his side. Roberto walked behind them and touched his friend's shoulder. He waved Angela and Edoardo over to the living area, and as they ambled off, he whispered something in Andrea's ear.

Andrea's shoulders slumped. His eyes darkened, and he pushed his hands hard against his face, blinking back tears. Maria ached for him.

Holding back her own tears, she tried to distract herself by staring at the cotton on the black couch. It was unstitched from overuse, and the rug underneath rolled up at the sides. Maybe she could help Lucia get some new furniture or she could get out her sewing kit and repair the stitching on the couch. Maybe she could give her the rug from Filippo's room.

Lucia's hand on her shoulder brought her back to the present, and she looked up into her friend's worried face. She forced a smile and followed Lucia to the cramped kitchen with its little bench space and narrow cupboards. She watched Lucia plate up macaroni with the deliciously-smelling sauce, then called to Angela who helped serve the pasta while Maria cut the home-made bread into bite-sized pieces. She turned to her friend.

"So where's Marco tonight?"

Lucia wiped her hands on an apron, taking a deep breath. "He's on the night shift."

As they sat down for dinner, Maria dug into the meal half-heartedly. She missed Salvatore and wondered if she'd done the right thing. Maybe she should've waited for him to sober up. Then they would've come home together. Maybe she could've gone to the church ceremony, which would have given him to time to sober. Maybe then he'd be fine. What was she thinking, just leaving him there? She left him with a virtual stranger. At least the young man seemed to be trustworthy. His girlfriend had proven to be when she'd driven them home.

"Are you okay?" Andrea asked.

Maria's heart whirled. "Fine, darling. Your father's not well, so he's being taken care of. He should recover soon."

"So where did that man take him?" Edoardo asked.

Lucia intervened. "Hey, you want to hear an interesting story?"

Roberto said, "I do, I do."

Angela nodded. "Of course, tell us."

"Well, it was on the radio news." Lucia chuckled. "This woman was robbed by some thug. She managed to hit him over the head with her frying pan and knocked him to the ground. Some guts, that woman."

Maria laughed. "My God. That's hilarious." Her tone turned serious. "There have been some robberies and attacks lately. Not that the police do much."

"Poverty, my dear," Lucia said. "It makes people do strange things."

Maria thought about poor Roberto's attack over a year ago. His arm was mostly healed but it had been a traumatic time for him.

They finished their food and were about to clear the table when a loud knock interrupted them. Maria walked to the door and wondered who it was, for Lucia wasn't expecting any visitors. She unlocked the door and gasped at seeing Salvatore, looking flushed and dishevelled. His face softened when she opened the door. She glanced over her shoulder at the children's anxious faces, then walked outside, closing the door behind her.

Salvatore quickly grabbed her around the waist and held her, but Maria didn't reciprocate. She stiffened and said, "What do you want? Haven't you caused enough damage?"

"Please, Maria. Forgive me. I'm sorry, but I honestly don't remember anything. I've sobered up, and the kind gentleman just told me—I'd hit you." He shook his head, pressing his fingers to his temples. "I cannot believe I did such a horrible thing. I'm so sorry."

Tears stung Maria's eyes. "You punched me, to be exact. You—knocked me to the ground without caring what you did."

He stroked her cheek and twirled a strand of her hair. "I would never hurt you intentionally, you know that. I—I just drank a bit too much, and I didn't know what I was doing. I love you deeply, Maria."

"Maybe you shouldn't come home tonight."

He frowned, then took her gently by the shoulders. "No, I'm your husband and I will never do what I did ever again. It was the alcohol. That's not me, you know that."

She moved back to distance herself. "Then you need help. Check in at the hospital."

Salvatore flinched. "I can stop on my own. I don't need the hospital."

Maria shook her head. "I don't believe you. You have to do this for yourself, and you have to talk to someone about Andrea's accident. Keeping things bottled up is not healthy. You haven't been yourself, Salvatore."

He edged closer to her, his hands back around her waist. "Will you give me a chance?"

"You hit me in the face. You really hurt me—deeply."

He nodded. "I know, but please let me make it up to you." He edged closer to her then slid his hands around the waist, holding her while massaging her back. She felt such deep stirrings, but she stepped back out of his grasp.

"Don't do that."

The look he gave her was like a magnet she couldn't resist. "Why don't we go for a walk? Clear our heads."

She nodded then turned back to close the door. As they walked, the warm scent of him, with its still lingering trace of the aftershave she loved, made her yearn for his touch. She couldn't give in to temptation. They had problems and they couldn't be solved simply by giving in to her womanly desires.

He took her hand and stroked it gently with his thumb. "I promise to stop drinking, Maria. I'm a man of my word. If I can do it in business, I can do it with alcohol."

Her heart raced as he held her hand, but she ignored it. "Why do you drink, Salvatore?"

He shrugged. "I don't know. Maybe it's a way to hide what I really feel." He stopped walking and they stood beneath a tree, towering in the darkness. He faced her, still holding on to her hand. "I know I have to learn to open up with my emotions, and I will. I need time to do that. Maria—only you can show me how to be a better person. You make me a better person." He started stroking her back, then her neck, and edged closer in. "I want you so much. I need you so much. I love you."

"I love you too."

"That boy I saw at the procession reminded me of Andrea and what I did to him. It really affected me—then I went to the bar and bought a bottle of wine. It helped me to forget what I did to my son for a while. I needed to forget."

"I'm sorry, but you need to forgive yourself. It was an accident. Speak to someone."

He nodded. "I'll talk to the priest."

"And you have to stop drinking. That's a must, Salvatore."

"I will, my darling. I will."

Salvatore looked at Maria, lingeringly. Then he suddenly pushed her against the tree and kissed her with fiery passion. She pulled back a moment, thinking she was crazy to do this, but her emotions confused her.

Salvatore stroked her cheek and drew her in again. Their tongues danced as Maria ran her hands through his hair and Salvatore played with her breasts underneath her blouse. His hands slid down her body. Then he took off her skirt and undergarment and spread her legs, touching her upper thighs. Oh God, how she loved his touch, but he was using sex as a way to make her forget. It was too soon, wasn't it?

He let go long enough to take off his pants. Then they continued to explore each other's bodies. Maria pulled back again, wondering if Salvatore would really stop drinking. What if he just told her what she wanted to hear? What if he was manipulating her just to come back home? Then again, maybe he really was telling the truth. He deserved a chance, didn't he? The children deserved to have a father.

As Salvatore brought her close, he took her hand and started kissing her over her chest, lingering with her flat belly while squeezing her nipples. He took off her blouse, then licked her nipples until they became erect. Maria's breathing quickened. She took control and stroked him across the chest and licked his earlobe. Kissing him hard on the mouth felt warm and sensual, and she became fully aroused. He was driving her crazy, and she couldn't stop herself. She was too far gone.

Salvatore took the reins again as he held her around the waist, exploring her mouth deeply with his. He lifted her knee then entered her and they climaxed simultaneously. Standing against the tree, they hugged each other in silence.

Maybe things would finally work out. Once he got the help he needed, Salvatore would be back to normal. She'd have him back.

Chapter 26

INSIGHT

Roberto's feet sank into mushy ground as he pushed Andrea forward in his wheelchair. The wind ruffled his hair and chilled his skin. Andrea was tired of being cooped up in the house so they had decided on a nature walk. Crows soared above as Roberto felt the weight of the wheelchair churning over loose stones, gravel, and dried grass, leaving tracks in the old dirt path. His breathing became laboured as he continued to push, but he struggled on. Eventually he stopped pushing and stepped in front of Andrea.

"What did you eat last night? You are so heavy," Roberto said.

Andrea threw his head back and laughed for the first time in a long while. "Ha ha, you're so funny."

"Can we stop? This is a good place—just listening to the trees speak to us."

Andrea continued to chuckle, and it brought a smile to Roberto's lips. "Aren't we the poet now?"

Roberto shrugged. "I aim to please." He hesitated. "We haven't had much time to talk about stuff."

Andrea turned his face up to the sky and cleared his throat. "What do you want to talk about?"

"Well—this. Your wheelchair. Your Papa."

Andrea looked away, but not before Roberto saw the tears. Andrea's breathing became shallow, and Roberto's with it, the silence between them growing as thick as the rustling trees.

"Andrea—I know it's hard, but you can talk to me. Don't shut me out."

Andrea's hands were shaking. "What do you want to know?"

Roberto knelt on the hard ground. "I don't know. Whatever you need to tell me."

Andrea's shoulders stiffened as he turned away. "I—I love Papa. What happened was—was an accident."

"But he was drunk when it happened."

Andrea shrugged. "It was still an accident."

"But he beats you."

Andrea straightened his shoulder. He turned and looked at Roberto straight in the eye. "My Papa loves me, and it's his job to discipline me."

Roberto sighed, knowing that Andrea didn't want to think badly of his father. That was understandable. He'd probably do the same if Andrea had accused his own father of such things. Of course, his own father would never have done them.

He let it go and pressed onward. "And how are you doing with the wheelchair?"

Andrea turned away, playing with the collar of his shirt. After a moment, he said, "It's something I might have to live with for the rest of my life."

Roberto felt sick in the stomach. "No, the doctor said you could get better in about six months. You have to believe that."

Andrea shook his head. "I don't feel anything in my legs, don't you see?"

"But you will. Just believe it."

Roberto didn't get a response but waited until Andrea spoke again. "Let's just keep walking, okay? I don't care how far we go. I just need to get far away for a while." Roberto nodded, clenched his hands over the handles of the chair, and began wheeling his friend down the dirt path. He decided he'd enjoy the scenic views as he passed the small stone houses, towering trees, majestic mountains in the distance, and people leading donkeys with crates on their backs. Everyone they passed managed a wave and a smile, but they'd sell your secrets if they could, just gossiping about you out of sheer boredom.

The wind became harsher and stronger. Roberto's arms began to ache. He tensed up his shoulders and ignored his struggle. It was nothing compared to what Andrea had to deal with every day. He thought about his friend's mental pain and wished he could ease it, but he could only support him as a best friend could. He was happy they were living together. He'd even noticed how his mother and Salvatore had started laughing together again. It appeared as if his stepfather had stopped drinking in the past month or so. Whatever his mother had told Salvatore was obviously working. He smiled at the thought that his mother was happy with Salvatore again. He wanted to protect her from pain, and knew that now things would sort themselves out.

Roberto had better use of his wrist, so he'd started his woodwork again. That was a blessing. He had even got Andrea to help him out with some custom made orders, which had only been one so far, but he could build on that. He was getting better at the woodworking every day and had even found himself eyeing the olive-wood box Papa had been making for Mama. He thought he was finally good enough to finish it. He was sure his father would be pleased.

The silence, so far unmarred by anything other than the breeze through the trees, was suddenly broken by the sound of two voices in the distance. Two men were standing in front of a tiny stone house that looked weathered and in need of repairs. One of the figures was Salvatore.

Roberto stopped the wheelchair behind a tree for a moment and looked on, his body shaking. He pressed a finger to his lips, and Andrea replied with a soundless nod. They stayed hidden behind trees, looking on. Why was his body shaking? It was only Salvatore talking to some man, but he looked familiar. Where had he seen that man before? Was he a friend of his Papa's? Was he from around here?

Roberto's reverie broke when Andrea whispered, "What's Papa doing over there? And why are you stopping?"

Roberto's feet were frozen to the ground. "We won't bother him. Is it okay if we turn back? We'll see him back home."

"Sure."

Roberto made no move to leave.

Salvatore planted his hands on his hips, shaking his head. The other man waved his arms and suddenly shouted, "Bastardo!" That voice sounded familiar, but where had

Roberto heard it? Salvatore bowed his head and closed his eyes. If only Roberto could hear what they were saying next, but they weren't shouting this time.

He saw Salvatore reach into his pocket and grab some lire. Hesitantly, he handed some notes to the man who threw back his head and laughed. As the man wagged a finger at Salvatore, his sleeve slid up his wrist, revealing a serpent tattoo. That tattoo!

Salvatore cast his head down and rushed off, but the man continued to stand at the door with his arms crossed, staring at Salvatore's retreating back.

Roberto couldn't breathe. His head felt heavy, and he reeled backward as if from the weight. Too dizzy to stand, he sank to his knees and held on to the handles of the wheelchair. It couldn't be. It just couldn't.

"What's wrong?" Andrea asked.

Roberto cleared his throat, feeling the weight of his body. "Nothing. I just need to rest for a while."

Andrea said nothing as they sat in silence. Roberto hoped that the man who was talking to Salvatore wasn't the same man who had attacked him with the bat and injured his wrist. He wished he wasn't also the man who had stolen their vegetables and locked him in the closet. What was the man planning to do now? Why was he talking to Salvatore?

Chapter 27

CONFRONTATION

The next day, Roberto walked to school and into the corridor with Andrea, but then turned back. The building was old with cracks in the walls, vinyl flooring, dirt and dust gathering in the corners, and small classrooms with tiny desks the books barely fit into.

"Where are you going?" Andrea asked.

"I have something to do. I can't be at school today so just let the teachers know I didn't feel well."

Andrea angled his head and put up his hands. "What is going on? Yesterday you seemed a bit strange and now this."

"Just do this for me, and I'll tell you when I can."

Andrea nodded, sighing, then wheeled himself into the small classroom.

Roberto watched him, his shoulders feeling tight from what he was about to do. He rushed out of the corridor and took a long walk into the centre of Eboli. He thought about what he was going to say to his stepfather. How could he be doing business with a man who did bad things? Why did he give that man money? Roberto was sick in the stomach and his legs felt weak as he dragged them across the dirt path.

He passed by an old man who smiled, a few children running late for school, out of breath, and a couple of men kicking a football into a tree like it was a goal post. As if he couldn't move fast enough, he ran for as long as his feet would take him, then slowed down to catch his breath. What was going on with Salvatore? Roberto wanted only the best for his mother, and if his stepfather was lying, he didn't know what he'd do. Roberto had to protect his mother from a man like that.

He'd always had the feeling that Salvatore couldn't be trusted. Now he might just get that confirmed. Assuming Salvatore even told him the truth.

The wind howled loud in his ears. He saw the rows of shops in the distance. Not too far now. He was close to the bakery where he'd speak to Salvatore. Where he'd get answers.

He paused just outside the bakery, his feet frozen to the ground. His heart raced, and his mind felt fuzzy. Even his throat went dry as he watched a group of men playing

Italian cards at an outside table. At another table, he saw a man and a young boy enjoying a sandwich, laughing at each other. It touched his heart as he thought about his own father. A father he could count on. A father who would never lie or do things behind a person's back.

He remembered some nice times he'd shared with Salvatore, but those were probably just a lie. Why had he trusted the baker in the first place? His hand wavered on the door handle. There was a part of him that didn't want the truth. What if the truth was so bad he wouldn't know what to do? He wasn't old enough for this. Was he?

Sucking in a long breath, then exhaling, he put one foot in front of the other and headed inside. He saw an older, chubby woman with greying hair smile while serving a customer.

"Well hello, dear Roberto," she said. "Salvatore's in the back. Go on in."

"Thank you," he said.

He cleared his throat as he passed by other workers baking bread and pastries, including panettone, brioche, and Italian donuts with sultanas. They were kneading, filling some up with custard and others with cream or sultanas. He loved all the sweets and enjoyed tasting them every time he came here. Not that he had much of an appetite now.

Salvatore mustn't have seen him, as he was huddled in a far corner of the tea room, drinking from a bottle, and then wiping his mouth.

"Salvatore," Roberto said.

Salvatore whirled around, gasping as the bottle slipped from his fingers. Bits of broken glass fell around him in a circle. He stared at the pieces then at Roberto.

"What are you doing here? Look what you made me do?"

Roberto didn't respond but quickly grabbed a cloth as well as a brush and pan from the store room. He got back into the tea room, bent down then swept up all the pieces of glass. He then wiped the floor with the cloth. Salvatore stood there frozen like a statue, staring at the ground.

Roberto felt nauseous. Salvatore was now drinking on the job. He thought he'd stopped drinking, but obviously not. What more could possibly go wrong?

When he cleared up the floor, he put the brush and pan away. He returned to the room where Salvatore was sitting at a table with his head bowed. His hands were shaking and his lips trembled as if he were cold.

Roberto sat beside him, toying with his hands and watching a man he only felt pity for. How could he behave this way?

"Why are you drinking?" Roberto said. "I thought you stopped."

Salvatore shrugged. "It was just a sip, nothing more."

"But your hands. They're shaking. I think you drank more than a sip."

Salvatore shook his head. "What are you doing here?"

Roberto watched as his stepfather looked far into the distance, almost as if Roberto wasn't there. The man was not his usual self, full of life and energy. This was a man who looked lost and wounded. Roberto almost felt guilty for having to talk about what he'd seen the other day, but he had no choice. Roberto had to protect his mother, and he'd move heaven and earth to keep her safe.

"I saw you a few days ago, with a man I know."

Salvatore suddenly looked up, frowning and fidgeting. "What are you talking about?"

Roberto took a deep breath. In one quick go, he explained what he'd seen in the mountains. Salvatore's face went white. He swallowed hard as his nails dug into his palms.

"That man just works for me at the bakery sometimes. I paid him what I owed him."

"What's his name?" Roberto asked.

Salvatore hesitated. "Federico."

"But he was the man that attacked me. The one that also stole our vegetables. How do you know him?"

"Well—well, like—like I said. I don't know what he did to you, but he works here."

Roberto's chest felt heavy. "But I've never seen him here. You're lying."

"Believe what you want, Roberto. I have no idea who he is, only that I gave him some work, and that's all I know."

"But why pay him at his home? Why not pay him here at work?"

Salvatore looked away, then turned back. "I didn't have the money then to give him, so I gave it to him there. Any more questions?"

He nodded. "Why don't you stop drinking?"

Salvatore rose from the chair. "And why don't you mind your own business? This has nothing to do with you. I can drink what I like, whenever I like. A few sips here and there do not mean a thing. So you get along to school now and never come to my work again without me knowing about it. Do you understand?"

Roberto was quiet as he got up to leave. There was no point speaking to a man who was almost drunk. Hopefully, he'd be better behaved once he got home.

Chapter 28

SEEING THE LIGHT

S traight after seeing Salvatore, Roberto headed to the mountains. A sudden shower drove him under a rocky overhang. He waited fretfully until it had subsided into a fine mist, then forged on. He was on a mission and needed answers. It was obvious that Salvatore wouldn't budge, so he tried another way. The man who had attacked him would have answers, but was he taking a risk? What if he got hurt again? Maybe he should be calling the police, but he knew they wouldn't believe him. It was his word against the man's. No, he'd take that risk for the sake of his family. If something happened to him, then so be it. It'd be on Salvatore's conscience.

The rain had turned the dirt path to mud. Roberto wiped the mist from his eyes and trudged through the grass at the edge of the path, careful not to soak his feet. His heart pounded and his fingers felt numb from the cold. He put his hands into his pockets and braced himself for the long walk. The mist veiled the mountain in grey, and he could barely see where he was going, but he had to keep walking. He had to understand how this man knew Salvatore.

The breath caught in his throat when the old house came into view. Not long to go now, but why wouldn't his legs move? He stayed still for a moment, knowing that he could be putting himself in danger. The man who lived here—Federico—was probably not a man you messed with, but Roberto was only there for answers. He didn't plan to go the police unless he had to.

Making his way forward, he swallowed and swung his arms to pick up his pace. He had to get this over with. Would the man be home? Maybe he had a day job. Did he really work at the bakery, or was that a lie?

A few metres away, Roberto took a few deep breaths and walked to the house. The door was in need of repair, with chipping paint and splitting wood. As he lifted his hand to knock, the door suddenly opened. A towering man with dark, almond-shaped eyes and an intimidating build stared down at him curiously. Then his fists clenched.

"Who the hell are you?"

Roberto gasped and drew back, blood pounding in his ears. "I think you know who I am."

The man hesitated. "Nope."

"I—I—saw you the other day, talking to my stepfather, Salvatore."

"So what of it? What's that to ya?" The man closed the door behind him and stood a few inches away from Roberto, his face hard. His breath smelled like dirt. Roberto moved back slightly. He could barely breathe.

"I need some answers." Roberto turned away for a moment, hoping someone was around if he needed rescuing. There was no-one. It was a deserted area. He shuffled his feet in the dirt.

The man pushed his head forward and grabbed Roberto by the shirt collar. "Listen—you get out of my face or I'll squash you like a peanut. You hear me?"

Roberto cleared his throat and ignored his rapid heartbeat. His body felt warm and his mind considered ways he could be killed right here, right now. "I'm not going to the police about you. I know you were the one who attacked me with the bat. I just want to know how you know Salvatore. That's all I want to know." He took a deep breath. "He paid you the other day. I saw him."

"So what? That's none of your damn business."

"Why was he paying you?"

"Why don't you ask him?"

Roberto sighed. "I did, but he told me you work at the bakery and he owed you money."

The man chuckled. "So I work at the bakery."

Roberto shook his head. "I've never seen you there."

"I work at odd times. You know I have other businesses. In fact, I'm off to one of them now, so if you don't mind."

"Please, just tell me the truth. I promise I won't go to the police. I only want to know about Salvatore. You see, he's married to my Mama, and I love her and want to make sure she's married a good person."

The man stared. "You got money?"

Roberto shook his head. "No, I'm just a kid. I go to school."

"Too bad. If you had money I could tell you whatever you wanted to know."

"But—"

The man put his finger over his temple, tapping it lightly. "You're a smart boy. I'm sure you could figure out a way to make some money."

Roberto thought about it. "I do woodwork. What if I made you something with my woodwork? You could sell it, make money."

"Thought you couldn't do it after your little injury?"

Roberto gasped, his vision blurry. "So you admit that you did attack me?"

He turned away. "I ain't admitting anything." He chuckled. "You can make me a wine rack. How soon could you do it?"

"It might take me a couple of weeks. I have to get the supplies."

"Well then, I guess I'll talk to you in a couple of weeks."

Roberto gestured with his hands. "No, please. I promise you that I will get it done. Just tell me the truth now."

The man gave it some thought then said, "Show me your pockets. I need something now. Then I'll tell you."

Roberto's stomach rolled. What had he got himself into? "Fine." He emptied his back pocket and gave the man a few lire. "Now tell me."

The man grabbed a cigarette and a lighter from his back pocket. He lit his cigarette then leaned his back against the shoddy door. He looked off into the distance as if remembering another time, another place. Roberto tapped his right foot on the ground, waiting in dread.

"I met Salvatore while your old man was still alive. He heard about me from a friend and knew that I did pretty much anything for some extra cash. A man's gotta survive, you know." He displayed an ugly smile. "Anyway, he got in contact with me and asked me to organise a robbery at your place. He didn't give me the reason but he wanted it done when he knew you'd be home alone. He left strict instructions for us not to hurt you, so we didn't."

Roberto felt nauseated. If there was a bucket next to him, he'd probably spew up right now. "What about my attack? Did he organise that too?"

The man looked up and nodded. "Sure did. Told me to hurt you on the wrist. Again, he didn't give me the reason for it, but he paid me well, so who was I to question why?"

"What about when he gave you money the other day?" Roberto asked, trying to ignore his rolling stomach and the jumble of thoughts that crowded his head. "Why did he pay you then?"

The man stared him down, not responding. "Now that's between him and me. That ain't none of your damn business."

"Did you do another job for him? Is that why he paid you?"

Redness swept over Federico's face. He seemed to grow suddenly larger. "If you tell anyone about this, I'll hurt your mother. Your stepfather's my bankroll."

Roberto didn't understand. "What do you mean?"

"He paid me not to tell your family what he did. Great Salvatore loves his new family," Federico said in a mocking voice. He was walking off, then turned back. "Now you get out of here. I don't want to see your kid face again."

Roberto headed in the other direction, constantly looking back to see if the man would follow him, but he didn't. He was off somewhere on the other side of the house. Slowly, Roberto's breath returned to normal.

As he walked, his feet sank into the ground. His legs felt like jelly, and his chest and shoulders ached. Tears ran down his face. With a shake of his head, he walked on ahead and tried to be strong for his mother.

Roberto wondered what he'd do with this information. He had to tell his mother for her own safety. Salvatore had hurt them all, so how could she forgive him for what he'd done? He would tell her today, but the timing had to be right. It had to be done in private, away from Andrea and his siblings. It was for the best.

Chapter 29

FLEETING HAPPINESS

Maria was on the sturdy wooden bench, crocheting a large piece of fabric to put on Lucia's couch, all the while thinking about her lovemaking with Salvatore a few days earlier. Her heart fluttered as she thought about his large hands touching her in all the right places. He knew how to please a woman, and it brought a smile to her lips as she ran the needle through the wool in a quick fashion.

A rustle outside made her look towards the door. It swung open and all the children hurried and laid their backpacks on the floor. Angela and Edoardo flung their arms around her, then headed to the kitchen. Roberto gave her a peck on the cheek and followed. Maria rose briefly to give Andrea a kiss, which he reciprocated before wheeling himself into the kitchen behind his siblings. She heard the refrigerator door open which was their usual routine after school. They were always hungry for a snack. Through the doorway, she saw Roberto wandering around the kitchen, a dark expression on his face. He seemed unusually subdued. What was going on with him?

She put down her crochet and headed to the kitchen. Edoardo was playing with Angela's hair while she playfully shoved him. Maria went to sit beside Roberto and watched as Edoardo pushed Andrea around the kitchen and Angela gave them each a slice of buttered bread.

"Everything okay at school today, darling?" Maria asked. Roberto stared but said nothing. "Roberto? Are you okay?"

He shrugged. "Something we need to talk about later, Mama. Not now."

"We can go into my room if you don't want the others to hear."

His shoulders seemed to weigh him down. "I think it's best we wait for Salvatore to come home."

Her breath quickened. "Does this have something to do with him?"

Roberto got up. "We'll talk later, okay?"

"Sure, darling." Maria tried to ignore the anxious flutter in her stomach as she wondered what news he had to share.

Maria went into the kitchen and prepared dinner. Lucia had given her rabbit from her husband's hunt, so they were having a feast tonight. It could be a celebration of a new journey; one in which Salvatore stopped drinking.

As the rabbit simmered on the stove, Salvatore arrived home. He greeted the children and approached Maria in the kitchen. He walked with a slouch, his words a little slurred. His eyes were bloodshot. Oh no, she thought. He bent to kiss her and she could smell the alcohol on him. Even after he promised he would stop.

Maria chopped the carrots fast, thinking about the children. She swallowed and felt bile rise in her throat as she continued to chop the carrots roughly. She'd deal with him later. For now, she wanted to enjoy a nice meal with her family.

As they sat down for dinner, Salvatore was unusually quiet and distracted. Roberto was quiet while the others chattered on about school and games they wanted to play. It was disconcerting that two of the men in her life were subdued. She noticed harsh glances from Roberto to Salvatore. What was that about?

"This rabbit's really good, Mama," said Edoardo.

"Yeah, it's nice and tender," said Angela.

"Thank you. It's nice to have meat on occasion." She realised too late what she'd said, and Salvatore's face became pale.

Andrea swung his arm forward to reach for a glass of water. He pushed forward his wheelchair but it wouldn't budge. The children were too busy enjoying their meal to notice that he needed help. When he finally grabbed the glass he accidentally spilled it, the water immersing into the remainder of the rabbit dish.

Salvatore suddenly looked up, shouting, "You stupid, stupid boy. Always the clumsy one, aren't you? Now, if only you could clean the damn mess up." He rose from his seat and stormed off into his room.

Maria drew back, shocked at his temper. "I'm sorry Andrea. Your father didn't mean it. Don't worry about it. It's only water."

Andrea blushed, and tears streamed down his cheeks. "I'm just useless. Papa's right. How can I do anything right in this stupid wheelchair. I'm no good to anybody."

Maria rose from her seat and walked over to his side. She embraced Andrea and stroked his hair. "Now don't go thinking that way. You have to believe that you'll walk again. The doctor said there is hope, but even if he's wrong, you're an intelligent boy. There are so many other things you can do with your mind."

Andrea shrugged. "It's just hopeless."

Maria shook her head. "Look, I know you liked being active with sports, but your Papa told me something else you like." She headed to the kitchen drawer and pulled out a hardcover book. "This is for you."

Andrea grabbed the book with a shaky hand. His face suddenly lit up. "How did you know I liked boats?"

Maria smiled. "Salvatore told me." Her heart warmed. "Maybe you could learn how to design boats in the future. There are so many choices in this world, so I'd like you to think about what you can do rather than what you can't do. Is that fair enough?"

Andrea's eyes welled up. "Yes, and thank you. I'll treasure this book."

Maria hugged him again, then pulled away. "Now no more talk about being hopeless. It's a positive journey from now on."

Andrea nodded.

As they were finishing their meals, Andrea chattered happily with all her children except Roberto. He smiled but had few words to say. His hands kept fidgeting and his eyes seemed to look into the distance, as if he was somewhere else.

After clearing up the dishes, Roberto approached Maria. "We need to talk. This cannot wait, Mama."

"Okay, we'll go in your room."

Maria followed Roberto into his room and closed the door. She waited as Roberto kept scratching at his skin, and looked down at the ground. He was obviously distressed about something.

"Darling, what's going on? You look like you've seen a ghost."

He sighed. "It's Salvatore."

Maria wasn't surprised. "What about him?"

Roberto looked away. "Salvatore is not the man you think he is."

Her heart beat quickened. "What do you mean? Start from the beginning, darling."

So there it started. Roberto explained what he'd seen and about Federico's story. Maria's heart broke as she listened without interruption. This had to be a nightmare. Surely, what Roberto said couldn't be true?

Maria headed to Roberto and hugged him tightly, stroking the back of his head.

"Oh darling, I'm so sorry you had to be caught in the middle of all this. You're just a child and you shouldn't have to get involved in his mess." She pulled away. "You did the right thing in telling me, but now I'll deal with it. I don't want you to worry about this."

"Okay, Mama."

"Good, now off to bed. Get some rest before school tomorrow."

As Roberto left for the bathroom, Maria slid onto the edge of the bed and let the tears stream down her face.

Chapter 30

THE TRUTH

That evening as Maria and Salvatore prepared for bed, she asked him a question.

"What?" Salvatore asked.

"You heard me." Her arms crossed against her chest. "Did you pay a man to hurt Roberto and steal our money and vegetables?"

Salvatore sat on the bed, looking defeated. "That's ridiculous."

Maria edged closer to him, standing. "Do not lie to me, for I won't stand for it. Already, you lied to me about the drinking, now if this is a lie too, I don't know—."

Salvatore's face became white, his eyebrows drawing together. "Maria, please."

"Please, what?" Her chest felt tight. She didn't want to believe anything Roberto had told her. Maybe that man Federico was lying.

"Do you really believe a stranger over me?"

"No, I believe my son and his instincts. Now please tell me the truth." She waited with bated breath, hoping that all of this was some kind of joke. Surely, this man she loved was not a monster, intent on hurting her son for his own selfish reasons. She hoped he'd tell her it was Federico who was the liar, not him.

Salvatore hunched over, shaking his head. She wanted to crawl under a rock and wait until this nightmare was over.

"If I tell you the truth, you're going to leave me, aren't you?"

Her heart skipped a beat, and her legs felt unsteady. She walked over to a chair near the door and sat, her body quivering. "Oh God, Salvatore. Please don't tell me you did this? What kind of monster would do this? Lie his way into the family. Oh God, no." She closed her eyes. She felt like she was being stabbed in the chest.

"I'm sorry, Maria, but—"

She looked up in fear. "You did do this, didn't you?"

He didn't look her in the eyes, but they were downcast. He nodded slowly.

She threw herself at him with her hands clenched and pounded him on the chest. "Bastardo! Bastardo! Cretino! Get out of here. I hate you so much. Get out! Get out!"

Salvatore grabbed Maria's hands and held them firmly. "Maria—please let me explain." She tried to pull her hands from his, but he was too strong, so she waited for him to loosen his hold before she stepped back away from him.

"What's there to explain? You hurt my son. You ruined our livelihood, and all because you wanted us to need you."

"Look, I told the man not to hurt his wrist that badly. I just wanted his wrist bruised so I could help him, be there for him. For you. Show you what kind of man I really am. One who loves you. I never meant for him to damage his wrist as much as he had. That was his decision."

"Oh—well that makes things so much better. You only wanted his wrist to be bruised. How touching!"

"Look, I love you Maria, and I just wanted to be there for you. Those vegetables were nothing. You know that I was able to help you out in the end. That's all I wanted."

"No, you wanted me to need you under pretence. Under manipulation. That's dishonest and sick. You're a monster, and I hate you." Tears welled in her eyes but she didn't wipe them away. "You dishonoured my husband, got my poor Roberto in trouble, and for what? Your selfish ego." She turned away. "Get out! Find somewhere else to live. With all the money you have, surely you can buy your way into anything." She turned away and started walking out of the room, then turned back. "I want you out of here tonight, so take whatever you need for now and leave."

"But Maria—what about us? We love each other."

"No— I loved a man who I thought was honest, devoted to his family. Now I realise it was all a lie. You don't love any of us. Not really." She left without turning back this time. She could no longer live life with lies and deception.

Chapter 31

TRAUMA

The following morning, Maria woke up with a splitting headache. Her legs felt like jelly as she walked into the kitchen to make herself an espresso. Her shoulders ached and her mind felt fuzzy. Pouring the coffee into the cup, she added a spoon of sugar and drank it down. Then she poured herself another cup, then another, and sat down, crying. Her body ached for Salvatore but her mind hated him with a vengeance. She almost wanted to kill him for what he'd done. It was something she'd never have believed about him, but it was true. At least he'd told her the truth in the end, but it had taken some time. He would never have told her the truth if she hadn't confronted him.

How would she break the news to the children? How could she make them understand without telling them the real truth? It wasn't fair for them to know. They didn't need to worry about such grown up things when they were so young. What about Andrea? She couldn't keep him away from his father, but she wanted to care for him. Salvatore was in no fit state to care for his son while drinking his sorrows away. If he wanted to help himself and care for his son, he'd need to stop drinking. Yet, she loved Andrea and could never think of parting from him.

The children eventually arrived at the breakfast table when Maria made them eggs and warmed up some bread. She laid out four plates and watched the children devour their food. Roberto watched his mother and headed towards her. He put his arm over her shoulder and kissed her on the cheek.

"I'm sorry, Mama. Are you okay?"

She nodded. "I will be. Don't you worry about me."

Andrea looked up from his food. "Where's Papa?"

Maria looked him in the eye, managing a fleeting smile. She moved forward and took his hand, stroking it. He smiled back, but with a concerned look in his eyes.

"Your father's not here, Andrea. We had a bit of an argument last night, so he'll be staying with a friend nearby. There are some things for us to work out, but you don't need to worry about it."

Edoardo put up his hand. "Hold up. What did he do? I mean, we know he's been drinking but what did he do this time? Leave you for another woman? Just kidding."

"Nothing like that. You don't need to worry."

Angela frowned. "But Mama, how can we not worry when you look so sad?"

"Well, that's part of life. It's okay to be sad sometimes. You can never shut off your feelings, Angela. Grown-ups cry too, you know."

Roberto squeezed Maria's shoulder. "It's okay, Mama. You have us."

She turned to Roberto. "Thank you, darling." Maria gathered them all in a group hug, warming her heart. She looked at them all with a reassuring smile, then said, "Okay, it's time to get to school."

They all headed off and left her there alone with her own private thoughts. She needed time alone to think, away from all distractions. Maybe some time with Lucia would cheer her up a bit. She might pay her friend a visit later.

After showering and dressing, she looked in the mirror and noticed the dark circles under her eyes. Her face looked pale and her hair was a tangled mess. She couldn't get it right today.

In spite of her yearning for Salvatore, she couldn't forgive him for what he'd done. It was unforgivable. It was like he'd cut out a part of her soul and fed it to the lions. How could he regain her trust? No, she wouldn't be ready to see him for a long time, if ever. Too much rage burned inside her, and she might never be able to put out the fire.

Maria thought about Federico, who was paid to do those horrible things, and wondered who could stoop so low for money. She knew there were criminals around. She just didn't want them in her village or near her children. She was scared for them. They were so vulnerable. Hope against hope, this man would never be paid to hurt them again. She was inclined to go to the police, but then she'd be implicating her own husband, and she couldn't do that. She was sure he was suffering without getting the police involved.

Maria was about to leave when she heard a noise. It sounded like someone at the front door. As she stepped quietly near the door, she could hear a tap on the wood.

"Is anybody there?" She asked. Suddenly, the noise stopped. Feeling queasy, Maria headed towards her bedroom. She had an uneasy feeling, so she decided to go out the back door into her garden. This was ridiculous, she thought. All these ideas in her head were making her believe that someone was trying to get into her house.

Shaking herself out of her reverie, she headed back around to the front of the house. It was probably a bird at the door. She was being ridiculous. No-one was trying to get inside. She had to leave to get to Lucia's.

Swinging open the front door, she shrank backward with a sudden gasp of fear. A strange man sat on the chair on her porch. "Who are you?"

He smiled but it wasn't a real smile. He was a towering man and looked very intimidating. "I'm a friend of Salvatore's, and have some business with him."

She stayed inside the house, ready to close the door. "Well, you can go to his bakery. He's not here."

Maria started to close the door, but the strange man beat her to it. He stopped the door with his foot, then scurried inside the house. He closed the door behind him.

Maria couldn't breathe. "What do you want?"

He approached closer to her, sneering. "Well is that any way to greet your husband's friend? I just want to talk, that's all."

Maria swallowed, goosebumps stippling her skin. Her legs felt weak and she looked around for a weapon. The lamp was too far away for her to reach. She edged her way closer to it but the man noticed and came nearer. He licked his lips and grinned.

"You are one gorgeous-looking woman. Nice curves too. Even your breasts, so round and ready."

Her breathing shallowed. "You know, Salvatore will be home any minute. He'll hurt you if you come near me."

"I saw him at work." He grabbed her by the shoulders. "I thought you might be lonely."

Maria's blood was boiling. "You're the bastard who attacked my son and stole our vegetables? It's you, isn't it?"

"What if it is?" He dug his thumbs in her shoulders. "My heart's crying out for you, darling. Come here."

Maria was trembling. She bolted for the door but he grabbed her from behind and pulled her towards the bench. His hand went over her mouth. She tried to break free from his hold but his strength overtook her. He punched her in the mouth hard, and she jerked back from the searing pain.

"Now you do as I say or I'll kill you. You might even enjoy it."

"Never. You'll never have me."

He drew out a switchblade stiletto knife from his back pocket. When he clicked the button, she tried to pull away at the sight of the pointy, silvery blade, after gouging his eye. He pulled back for a moment but managed to stop her from leaving. "You bitch!" This time he punched her in the eye. "Do that again, and I'll use my knife. Better yet, I'll hurt your kids." He chuckled. "I will kill you if you give me a reason to, so you'd better do as I want."

His breath was a sickening warmth against her face. It smelled like onions. As he leaned in, he whispered what he would do to her children.

Maria closed her eyes, tears rolling down her cheeks as she tried to take her mind to another place. Her body shook. He started to touch her breasts, his hands roaming down her body. It had to be over soon, she thought.

Chapter 32

A BAD FEELING

Roberto was in school, his mind filled with worry as he listened to his teacher ramble on about the Italian verbs. Who cared about this? His goal was to do craft work. Did he really need to know the rules of grammar?

His mind cast back to the night before when he gave his mother the news about Salvatore. It was heartbreaking to see the pain on her face, the despair. He was the cause of that despair. Yet he had had no choice. It was for her own good, and better now than later. Either Salvatore would have to change or he'd be out of their lives forever. Roberto would miss living with Andrea, but he had to think of his mother's happiness.

When it was time for their break, Roberto thought about his dream from last night. In it, all he could see was a face getting closer and closer, threatening to hurt him, but he couldn't see if it was Salvatore or Federico. He'd been helpless, his body frozen. Remembering the dream, he felt uneasy. Had he done the right thing confronting Salvatore and telling his mother? Maybe he'd made things worse. Who knew what Salvatore was capable of when he got drunk? What if he hit his Mama again?

The shuffling of papers and the scrape of chairs on the hardwood brought Roberto back to reality. His hand clenched around his pencil as a sudden dread came over him. He needed to know his mother was safe. He scooped his belongings together as his classmates surged towards the door, where Andrea lingered, waiting for him.

"I have to get home," Roberto said.

Andrea knit his brows and wheeled himself into the corridor. He was beginning to adapt to the wheelchair, and Roberto was grateful for that. "Why?"

"I just need to check on Mama. I'll see you at the house." He ignored Andrea's sigh and dashed outside, hurtling down the path towards home. He sprinted as fast as he could, out of breath, but he didn't care.

Ignoring passersby, Roberto told himself he was probably worrying for nothing. Surely, his mother was okay. He was just worried about the man who had hurt them. He ran faster anyway, remembering a saying his father had often used: Better safe than sorry.

Grass rustled beneath his feet as he ran. He pressed a hand to a stitch in his side and forced himself to run on. The house came into view, and he slowed down, gasping for breath. The house was quiet but the door was slightly open. That was strange. Mama never left the door open. With a pounding heart, he banged the door open and ran into the house.

The room was dark, the curtains pulled. His mother huddled on the bench, eyes glazed, hugging herself. Despite the blanket over her, she was shivering. He drew closer, trying to even out his breathing. She didn't even look up. He rested on the bench beside her, noticing the dried blood around her swollen lip. Around her eye there was bruising. She looked frail and distant, as if her mind was thousands of miles away. He felt dizzy with a fluttery feeling in his belly, but he had to ignore it and help his mother. She needed him now. He had to be strong for her.

Perched on the edge of the bench, he slid his arms around her. She stiffened, her mouth opening in a silent protest.

"Mama, it's me. Roberto. Are you okay?"

Her gaze swung wildly towards him. Then her body softened and her eyes cleared. "Oh, Roberto." Her voice broke, and her eyes filled with tears. Roberto didn't know what to say or how to make her feel better.

They held each other for a long moment. Then Roberto pulled away and made her sit up. "I'm sorry, Mama, but you need to tell me what happened. We need to go to the police with this."

"No!" She shook her head, then drew in a calming breath. "No, darling. We can't do that. Just leave things be. I'll be fine, don't you worry."

Roberto felt a sudden rush of guilt. This was all his fault. He should never have left her alone.

"I will kill Salvatore," he said.

He started to rise, but she laid a hand on his arm. "It wasn't Salvatore."

Roberto's stomach sank. If it wasn't Salvatore—"Was it a tall man with dark eyes that came here? Did he hurt you?" His mother's eyes told him it was. "That's who told me about Salvatore—the one who attacked me, Mama. Don't you see, he's done too much to this family. We need to call the police."

His mother laughed, but it sounded forced. "The police. It'll make things so much worse, Roberto." She looked away. "There are some things you wouldn't understand. I couldn't bear it."

"What did he do to you, Mama?"

His mother focused on the ground. "Nothing you need to know."

His stomach churned as he realised what she was telling him. His hands curled into fists. He wanted to kill that man.

Chapter 33

SEEKING HELP

L ater in the day, Maria drank a cup of espresso that Roberto made. He wiped her face with a warm facecloth and cleaned the dried blood from around her lip. She refused to take the blanket off herself, but managed to sit up. Her breathing was erratic as her mind took her to that dark moment where she'd lost control of her life.

Maria rose from the couch and walked gingerly to her bedroom to grab a coat. Her feet felt heavy and her body ached. She made herself ignore the pain and bruising around her private areas. One foot in front of the other, she told herself. One step at a time.

She pulled on the coat, wincing at the searing ache in her back and shoulders. Halfway to the front door, Roberto stopped her.

"What are you doing?" His hand closed over her shoulder.

"I have to see Lucia."

"Why? You're not well, Mama."

"I have to see Lucia," she repeated. "She can contact her lady friend close by. Someone who can help me heal my wounds."

"Is she a doctor?"

"No, she's a kind of nurse. She probably knows more than doctors."

Roberto let go of her shoulder and looked at the ground. "Okay, but I'm coming with you."

They trudged towards Lucia's house. It wasn't far, but today it seemed like a long way. Maria hoped her friend would be home. Lucia normally worked early in the morning and got home early in the afternoon.

The pain stopped her in her tracks in front of Lucia's house. Roberto put his arm around her and helped her walk the few paces to the door. After a moment's hesitation, she knocked on the door, forcing a smiled when Lucia answered.

"Maria? Are you okay?"

"I'm fine. I...I need to talk to you privately."

Lucia nodded, then swung open the door and let them in. The smell of lavender filled the air as they walked into the living room. The living room was dark and cold, but Lucia drew the curtains to let in the rays of daylight. Maria glanced around, not yet ready to meet her friend's gaze. She noticed fresh lavender in a vase.

Lucia handed Roberto a magazine. "Here, darling, go sit in my room. You can read this." He gave Maria a worried glance, then at her nod, rolled the magazine into his fist and disappeared into Lucia's bedroom.

Maria hugged herself. She'd tried to hold herself together for Roberto's sake, but now she felt cold and worn out. She could barely lift her legs.

Lucia led her to the couch and eased her down onto the cushion. "Now, dearest Maria. Tell me what happened."

Maria folded her hands tightly in her lap. Through a haze of tears, she recounted her horror story. When she was finished, she looked up. Lucia's face was ashen. She glanced away, hand over her mouth, as if unable to meet Maria's gaze. A sob caught in Maria's throat. Had telling Lucia been a mistake? Fresh tears stung her eyes, and she wiped them away with the back of her hand.

Lucia hurried to the end table, snatched some tissues, and thrust them at Maria. Her eyes blazed with love and indignation.

"My God, you have to go to the police."

"No police. It'll make things worse for the family."

Lucia drew back. "Are you mad, woman? This man raped you and held a knife to your throat. He could've killed you. You need to call the police. He might come back for you."

Maria shook her head. "Then I'll be ready for him. I'll kill him myself, but I won't drag my family through this shame, this scandal. I can handle it, but I won't expose my children to that. I just can't."

She searched Lucia's face for some kind of censure or judgement but found only sympathy. Finally, Lucia nodded. "I understand, but I think you should tell Salvatore." Maria was silent. "Maria? Don't you think you should tell Salvatore about this?"

Maria shrugged. Her feelings for Salvatore were far too complicated to discuss right now. She could hardly describe them to herself. "We're separated."

Lucia sat down on the couch and took Maria's hands in hers. "Oh, honey, why? What happened?"

Maria explained the situation, and again saw the shocked expression on Lucia's face. It felt good to let it all out, to be comforted by her friend.

"I need your help, Lucia."

Lucia stroked Maria's hand. "Anything darling."

"That lady friend of yours. The one with the gift. I need her to check me. She has a way of knowing about these things."

Lucia frowned. "You mean, pregnancy? You think you could be? Pregnant?"

"I don't know." Maria turned away in shame.

Lucia said softly, "I'll go get her right now. You wait here, darling. I won't be long."

Maria closed her eyes and took slow, deep breaths, trying to calm herself down. She lay down on the couch for a moment, resting. What would the lady say? If she was pregnant, she'd be completely shamed. It'd be such a scandal that no-one in the village would ever believe she was raped. They'd think she went looking for it willingly. Maybe she could pretend the baby was Salvatore's. Nobody would have to know the truth. It was too shocking, too scandalous. No, it was better to save the family from the real truth.

She thought about going to the police for what that man had done to Roberto, but there was no evidence of wrongdoing. Besides, then she'd be getting Salvatore in trouble as he was the organiser of two crimes. She couldn't believe he'd done such a horrible thing to Roberto, a stepson he should've loved and protected like his own.

From outside, she heard women's voices, followed by the creaking of the door. Footsteps resounded in the house. Maria lifted herself into a sitting position and looked up to see an old woman strolling inside. She had a pointy nose, hunched shoulders, and wrinkly hands. Her build was short and petite, her eyes the bluest Maria had ever seen. A beauty in her younger days, no doubt. She must've been at least eighty years old. Was her gnarled body the result of all the tragedy she had seen in her years of living? Maria took a deep breath and ignored the anxiety fluttering in her stomach. Now was the moment of truth.

Chapter 34

THE FUTURE

Lucia came into the room and gave Maria a reassuring smile. "Maria, this is Isabella. I've never used her services but I've heard how accurate she is with her impressions."

Maria took a deep breath and swallowed while Isabella sat beside her on the couch. Lucia sat in the armchair, and crossed her arms.

Isabella put Maria's quivering hand in her own. "You must relax, my dear—you need to be open enough for me to see."

"I'm sorry," Maria said. She took a few more deep breaths and closed her eyes, her body slowly sinking into the couch. Aches and pains in her back and stomach almost deterred her, but she pushed through.

Maria opened her eyes, feeling slightly soothed by the woman's soft hand, but when Isabella let go of her hands and touched her stomach, Maria cringed. What if she was pregnant? How would she cope with the scandal of how she fell pregnant in the first place?

She watched Isabella purse her lips, close her eyes, and hum to herself. The frail body started to shake. Then she took her hands off Maria's stomach as if they'd been burnt. Isabella took some deep breaths then opened her eyes, focusing behind Maria and into the distance.

Maria waited and waited, a knot in the pit of her stomach. What could be haunting the old woman? She imagined her stomach swelling, imagined the squall of a red-faced newborn. If Isabella told her the worst; if there really was a child, could she love it?

Isabella said, "I see death."

Maria gasped, pulling back. Her vocal chords knotted. No, that couldn't be right. She couldn't have heard right, could she?

"Death is around you," the old woman intoned.

Maria leaned forward. "Who dies?"

Isabella opened her eyes. "We are not meant to know—because we cannot stop it. It is meant to be."

Bile rose in Maria's throat. Death. One of her children? If she'd ever lost any of them, she couldn't bear it. She thought she might vomit.

Maybe that wasn't what the vision meant. If death was around her, maybe she'd be a witness to something; an event of some kind. It didn't have to involve her family, did it? Or maybe there was a baby, and it would die in her stomach. Maybe before anyone else even had to know she was pregnant. She waited for more, and when it didn't come, she touched the back of Isabella's hand.

"Am I pregnant?"

Isabella hesitated, closing her eyes again. She shook her head. "I do not see a baby, but I do see a new life, a new beginning, and—someone who learns from his mistakes."

"Who is that?"

"I cannot tell, but trust your instincts."

After a few moments, the woman kissed Maria on the cheek. "I wish you well." She moved towards Lucia and kissed her on the cheek too. "You will soon have a baby," she said to Lucia who gave a wide-eyed, nervous giggle. "Good luck." She left them both speechless.

Closing the door, Lucia shook her head in wonder, then turned to Maria and hugged her. "Good news about you not being pregnant."

Maria smiled. "And great news about you soon having a baby. She's usually right about the future, isn't she?"

Lucia nodded, one hand absently touching her stomach. "Almost always. But what's that about death? That's pretty scary."

Maria cleared her throat. "I'm probably just a witness to death, that's all."

Lucia patted her on the shoulder. "Are you going to talk to Salvatore about what happened?"

Maria thought about her husband's selfish actions. "Didn't you hear what I said before? He hurt my son, and I can never forgive him for that."

Lucia looked away. "Never is a long time."

Maria felt her eyes narrow. "He can rot in hell, for all I care. He'll never have any part of me again. He got his chance when he told me he'd stopped drinking, and lied to me about it. Now this—it's unforgivable. He's a liar and manipulator, and doesn't deserve to be a part of our family." She wished she had appreciated Giovanni a lot more.

She left Lucia and stalked towards the bedroom down the end of the hall. She opened the door and saw Roberto sitting on the bed, reading the magazine. As Lucia came in behind her, Maria went over and tugged her son by the hand. "Let's go, darling."

Roberto set the magazine aside and swung his legs over the edge of the bed. His questioning gaze flicked from her to Lucia. "What's going on?"

Lucia looked to Maria for a response. When none came, she said, "Nothing. Your mother's just tired."

Tired. Maria stifled a laugh. She was beyond tired, but she didn't argue. Instead, after they'd both given Lucia a quick hug, Maria steeled herself for the walk home.

When they arrived, the children were already home from school and Salvatore sat at the table, laughing with Edoardo and Andrea. Angela was cutting zucchini on a chopping board, listening in on their conversation.

Maria glanced at Roberto, who stood beside her, mouth open, as if not knowing what to do. Salvatore looked up, half-smiling. Then his gaze swept her bruised face and the smile faded. He headed towards her but she moved away, and said brightly, "Hello everyone. I need to have a shower." She turned to Angela. "I won't be long, darling, then I'll help you with dinner."

She hurried into her room, tears overflowing. Why was he here? He didn't deserve to be here? If Salvatore thought he could be suddenly forgiven, he was sadly mistaken.

Chapter 35

CONFLICT

January 1950

Three months later, Roberto, Edoardo, and Angela sat in the back pews of the church in the city centre with their mother. Andrea kept his wheelchair still behind their seats. He fumbled with his prayer book, ignoring churchgoers who greeted his mother. Andrea's face flushed each time the heavy doors opened, a gust of wind ushering in each new arrival.

The sermon by the priest was enough to put Roberto to sleep but he watched his mother seemingly focused on every word.

He overhead one of his mother's older friends ask, "Let's have coffee, dear. It's been a while." She was seated in front of them, wearing a scarf over her head.

His mother said, "I'd love that."

"Just come by next week."

"Okay," Maria said.

The woman smiled and turned her head to the front.

Roberto was happy that his mother was able to keep busy with her friends. She needed the distraction. After what had happened with Salvatore, he doubted his mother would ever forgive him. He only wished that Federico could be punished for what he did.

The songs and final prayers brought him back to life as he stood, and then knelt with the others. He bowed his head and prayed that his mother would be okay. He prayed that she'd manage on her own, without Salvatore.

Angela touched her mother on the shoulder as if she sensed Mama's pain while Edoardo made funny faces to make his mother laugh. Rather than laugh, she shook her head and told him to be quiet. Andrea fidgeted and looked far into the distance. He obviously hated being around people, given his wheelchair.

Salvatore had agreed to let Andrea stay with her family until Andrea forgave him, and Roberto was happy to have him. Salvatore had visited the house only a few times in the last few months, probably wanting to give them space, but the conversation was always awkward. Andrea would probably never forgive his father.

When the mass ended, people slowly walked down the aisle row by row, some of them smiling at Roberto and his mother. He smiled back, but wasn't in much of a mood to feel anything but despair. He still thought about Federico, and how he was roaming free after what he did to them, but he hadn't seen him around.

If ever Federico hurt them again, he'd go to the police then. If only they could contact the police, but his mother outright refused. Salvatore still didn't know what had happened to his mother, as she had refused to tell him.

As Roberto left the church with his family, his shoulders sagged and his stomach turned at the sight before him. His fists clenched and blood came rushing to his face. Federico was standing in front of a pole across from a store waving at him. An uncontained rage came over Roberto and he charged at Federico, kicking him in the right knee then the left. Federico cursed and tried to grab him but Roberto ran around a tree, then grabbed some stones and threw them at the big man. They landed in the dirt at Federico's feet. Federico didn't flinch but shook his head, chuckling, and charged.

Roberto turned to run, but Federico's fingers snagged his collar and hauled him back. Roberto squirmed to get away as Federico's arm swung back to wound up for a punch. Roberto heard his mother cry out. Federico froze in mid-punch and turned his head towards Mama. She was holding back Angela and Edoardo. Edoardo's arms were swinging but his mother held on to him tight with one arm while Angela tugged against the other and cried. Poor Andrea stared in confusion. The sneer on Federico's face sent another wave of rage surging through Roberto. He stamped hard on Federico's foot. The big man roared and loosened his grip, and Roberto bolted towards a strip of shops close to the bakery.

"You idiot!" Federico yelled."You think you can hurt me?" He rubbed his foot and limped towards Roberto, who ran into his stepfather's bakery and ran headlong into Salvatore.

"What are—"

"Help me, please. That man Federico—he's trying to hurt me."

Roberto pulled his stepfather by the arm. Then understanding flooded Salvatore's face, and he jogged past Roberto. Federico was waiting. He lunged past Salvatore, grabbing a handful of Roberto's hair. Roberto scratched at Federico's hands but the man held tight. Roberto's scalp throbbed and burned. He was yanked upwards by his hair. Then the fingers loosened, and Roberto stumbled backwards. Salvatore had both arms around Federico's chest. He pulled the big man backwards and flung him away from Roberto. Roberto propped his hands on his knees, panting.

Salvatore turned to Federico. "What are you doing here? And why are you hurting Roberto?"

Federico moved closer to Salvatore, inches from his face. "Your stupid son kicked me in the knees for no reason."

A crowd had gathered. Salvatore looked around the community of staring people, then put up his hands and turned to those watching. "There's nothing to watch here. Please go about your business."

Reluctantly, the crowd dispersed. The two men stared each other down.

"Roberto!" Mama called. Roberto looked up to see his mother running towards him. She grabbed him sternly by the arm, avoiding the gazes of Federico and Salvatore.

"You get here now, Roberto. What are you doing?"

Roberto shook his head. "No, Mama. This stops now. You have to tell Salvatore the truth about this man."

Salvatore edged closer to his mother. He tried to take her by the hand but she yanked it away, and backed closer to her son. The others stared on. Andrea wheeled himself closer and said, "Do you know this man, Papa?"

Salvatore's face reddened. He rubbed his cheeks with the back of his hand, closing his eyes for a moment. He drew back but nodded slightly.

"Yes, son, I do," he said softly, then turned towards Federico. "What is going on here? What have you done now?"

Federico chuckled. "What have I done?" He looked at the family. "What have you done to this poor family?" He threw back his shoulders and counted off on his fingers. "Let's see what you did. First, you force me to steal their vegetables, then you get me to injure Roberto's wrist so he's out of action for a while."

Andrea turned to his father. "What is he talking about, Papa? That's not true, is it?" Silence. "Papa? That's not true what he said, is it?"

Salvatore avoided his son's gaze, focused on the ground. Silent tears fell down his face. Quickly, he brushed them away and turned towards Andrea. "I acted out of love for Maria, but I know now it was wrong. I will never do anything like that again. You have to believe me."

Andrea stared hard into his father's eyes. "I am ashamed to call you my father." He wheeled himself away and after a moment, Mama took Angela and Edoardo by the hands and followed him.

Roberto took a deep breath. He had to tell Salvatore the truth. He had to protect his mother, and this was the only way he knew how. He could no longer carry the burden alone. As much as he didn't like what Salvatore had done, he needed the man's guidance. Roberto waited for the others to leave, then said,

"This mad man came over to the house and—hurt Mama."

Salvatore blinked, staring at Roberto. "What?"

"A few months ago, he came over to the house and—and had his way with my mother. She didn't want me to say anything, but I had to tell you."

Federico leaned forward, sighing. "Listen, she came on to me. I just came over to the house and asked for you. She started kissing me, then it just sort of happened. It was as much her as it was me."

Salvatore clenched his teeth then his fists, his face turning a bright red. Then he punched Federico in the face.

Federico staggered back and hit the ground hard, eyes rolling up until only the white showed. Then he climbed unsteadily to his feet and shot Salvatore a venomous look. "You'll pay for that. Dearly."

Salvatore punched him again and again in the face until blood soaked his shirt and his eye turned black. Federico tried to block the blows with his hands, but his strength was no match for Salvatore's. If Roberto didn't do something, Salvatore would end up killing the man.

"Stop! Salvatore, stop." Roberto leapt forward and grabbed Salvatore by the arms, pulling him back with all his strength. Salvatore stepped back, breathing hard.

Federico slowly staggered to his feet, then shot forward, punching Salvatore straight in the eye. Salvatore reeled back, his shoulder blades thumping against the door of the bakery. Roberto ran to him.

"Are you alright?"

Salvatore nodded, wincing as he prodded the bone beneath his eye with a fingertip. Roberto looked up, realising that the villagers had gathered again, staring with their eyes and mouths wide open. The fight obviously brought them back. There was no sign of Federico.

Chapter 36

ESTRANGEMENT

Roberto watched the police walk out the door early on Sunday morning. He had just been questioned about Federico with his mother by his side. His chest felt tight as he thought how Federico was missing and might not be punished. He hoped the police would find him. He rubbed his eyes, saw his mother crying at the kitchen table, and sat beside her.

"Are you okay?"

She kept her head down, wiping away her tears. "Oh darling, why did you get Salvatore involved? Now he went to the police, and they asked me about him." She looked up with red, swollen eyes. "I never wanted this to come out."

Roberto took his mother's hand. "But, Mama. That man deserves punishment. Why should he be allowed to hurt someone else?" His mother didn't respond. She sipped the remainder of her coffee then rose from the table, cleared her throat, and rubbed her hands together.

"Enough of these morbid thoughts." She managed a smile. "Today, you'll be helping me make the tomato sauce. Wake the others, and let's get ready."

He forced a smile in return, realising that she wanted to get things back to normal. "Do we have enough tomatoes, Mama?"

She nodded. "We grew a lot of them, and Salvatore bought the rest."

Roberto walked quickly to wake up the others. "But it's Sunday." Edoardo groaned "Why can't we sleep in?"

"We stopped making sauce after Mama died," Andrea said.

"Well, we're doing it again," Roberto said. "It's loads of fun, so get up."

He left the room and walked into the backyard where his mother had set up a table for the mincer with a bucket underneath. Crates of tomatoes filled the barn so he carried them and laid them on the ground near the mincer. His mother had put some tomatoes into a pot to boil before mincing them up. Roberto loved to watch the juice of the tomato come out into the bucket while the skin and core fell into another bowl from another part of the machine.

He heard footsteps behind him as he grabbed more crates from the barn. It was Edoardo, pushing Andrea's chair on the uneven grassy ground.

"What can I do?" Andrea asked.

Roberto set down another crate and turned to his friend. "You can go through those tomatoes and sort out the good ones from the bad ones." He placed some of the tomatoes into a bowl and let Andrea sort them out from the table.

Angela arrived, sighing. "It's just too early for this." She kissed her mother on the cheek and sighed again. Blinking away sleep, she helped her mother ladle the tomatoes into the mincer. Roberto watched as the juice filtered out, pouring into the bucket. As he needed a laugh, he grabbed the skin and the bad bits from the other part of the machine and threw it at Andrea, grinning. The bad bits landed on his face, making Andrea shake his head.

"If I could run, you'd be dead by now," Andrea said.

"Hey, stop that. We're here to work, Roberto," his mother said.

Roberto turned serious then gave his mother a full bowl of tomatoes to boil.

Angela grabbed some jars and bottles from the barn to put the sauce into. Edoardo kicked around a soccer ball almost knocking down the bucket of sauce. His mother said, "Hey, Edoardo stop that! You nearly ruined our sauce. Now come over here and help."

Edoardo smirked. "Fine." He put the soccer ball away then emptied the bowl with the tomato skins into their garden for fertiliser.

Angela and Roberto were filling up the bottles with tomato sauce, dirtying their tops in the process. Roberto thought it looked like they'd been involved in a bloody battle.

After finishing up a whole crate of tomato sauce, the next batch of tomatoes was put into the machine. Mama grabbed a handful of tomatoes and had switched on the machine when she was interrupted by a strong voice.

"Can I help?" Salvatore looked over at all the children with a half-smile.

"What are you doing here?" Mama asked.

"I wanted to see how you were all doing." Salvatore walked over to Mama, and whispered. "Can we talk?"

She continued putting in more tomatoes, using a long stick to press the tomatoes into the machine. Salvatore was about to add more tomatoes but she shrugged him away.

"I don't need your help, and no—we cannot talk. There is absolutely nothing to talk about."

"Please, Maria. Whatever I did I know it was a mistake—I'd like to make it up to you." He turned to

Roberto. "It's been three months, and like I've repeated many times, I never meant for Roberto to get hurt like he did. I didn't order that. Federico just made up his own mind to injure him further."

Her gaze turned to the children. Then she pulled him inside the barn with the door slightly open. Roberto crept closer to the barn and listened. He wasn't even sure what he hoped for. Part of him had grown to love Salvatore, and hoped he could be part of their lives again, but another part thought that would just be asking for betrayal.

"You're a joke," Mama was saying. "You have no morals whatsoever, and you don't really know what love is. It's not about manipulation or lies, but about honesty and trust. I no longer trust you."

"But do you still love me?"

"Love has no relevance if I do not trust you. Can't you see that?"

Their approaching footsteps warned Roberto, who hurried back to his place and carried on with his duties. Salvatore came out first and turned to his son, who ignored him. "Andrea, I am so sorry. You know how much I love you". He looked at the other children, and motioned with his hands. "All of you. What I did was wrong. Can you please forgive me?"

Andrea's lips formed a cold, hard line, then he turned away. "I'm sorry Papa! You need to leave."

Salvatore's eyes filled. He fixed his sorrowful gaze on each of them in turn, then slowly nodded and walked away.

Roberto watched him leave with pity in his heart. Salvatore looked defeated and lost, but he did seem genuinely sorry for what he'd done. Roberto remembered all the times Salvatore had helped the family out, and he was grateful. Then he wondered: Had any of it been real? He remembered the time Salvatore showed him how to play soccer, touching his shoulders to lift his posture and teaching him how to kick with focus. When Roberto kicked the ball, it landed on Salvatore's stomach. He doubled over and then laughed at Roberto, saying 'now you're almost a soccer player'. Salvatore had patted him on the back with a smile. Roberto believed that was real. They had a connection, but was it enough?

Chapter 37

TAKEN BY SURPRISE

The following evening, Maria finished washing up after dinner. Angela dried her hands on a tea towel then hugged her mother.

"What was that for?"

Angela smiled her gorgeous smile. "I can see you're sad because of Salvatore."

Maria stroked her daughter's cheek. "I'm fine. Don't you worry about anything. Now, go and do your homework." She shooed her daughter out of the kitchen.

Maria dried her hands and looked out the kitchen doorway. Roberto, Edoardo, and Andrea sat in the living room finishing off their homework. Maria watched them, feeling blessed that her family was united. They had supported her all the way, and she was grateful for them. Yet, there was a feeling of uneasiness.

If only the police had caught Federico, she'd feel safe. She cast her mind back to the way he'd whispered to her all the things he'd do to hurt her children. It made her sick to the stomach. He was a madman and needed to be caught soon. The thought of his attack reminded her of Lucia's friend, Isabella. She was bothered by Isabella's prediction about death surrounding her. If death was around her, she hoped that God would save her family.

Feeling the weight of the world on her shoulders, Maria took out her crochet from a large bag then sat at the kitchen table, working on the piece. With her head down, she heard a noise from outside. That uneasy feeling came over her again so she rose and checked that the door was locked and the windows were secure. Roberto turned to her.

Roberto looked up at her. "Are you okay, Mama?"

"Of course, darling. Get back to your homework." Looking through the window, Maria noticed a storm brewing. She hugged herself, rubbing her upper arms. It was just the wind she'd heard, nothing to worry about.

Strolling back to the kitchen, she rubbed the tightness from her shoulders and upper back and sat back down. Her mind wandered as she crocheted her piece. Suddenly a bang came from the bedroom. Her crochet slipped from her lap as she moved towards the sound. The boys pushed their books aside and followed her, the pitter-patter of their feet behind her. With a chill in her heart, she hurried into Angela's bedroom.

Angela turned and held up her hands. "Sorry, Mama. I accidentally dropped my books."

Maria breathed a sigh of relief. "Not to worry, darling. Carry on." She smiled to herself as they all returned to the living room. She was worried over nothing, but then again she'd been through a lot. It was okay to be a little on edge and worried. If only the police had found Federico, she thought again. She'd probably sleep better. Surely he was long gone by now. He wouldn't dare show his face here again, knowing that Salvatore and the police would take care of him.

After the children had gone to bed, Maria made herself an espresso and read an Italian magazine. She was starting to feel tired so she drank down her coffee then switched off the lights in the kitchen. Walking in the dark, she fumbled for the bedroom switch and clicked on the lights so she could prepare for bed. She was physically exhausted from making the tomato sauce yesterday, but at least now they had a full stock to last them for a while. Yawning, she pulled on her nightgown and turned off the light.

As she was dozing off, something made her jump. A sound coming from the kitchen? Was it footsteps? Had Salvatore decided to show up for some sick reason? Her heart felt tight. She took a long breath and counted backwards from ten to one. There was nothing there. It was only her imagination. She turned on the bedside lamp, a heavy brass lamp that had once been her mother's and listened. Nothing.

Maria had started to doze off again when other noises jolted her out of a half-slumber. They made her skin crawl. Definitely footsteps. The footsteps seemed to edge closer. Then a scratching sound came from the door. She flung off the blankets and tiptoed to the door. Her breath sounded too loud in the stillness of the room.

The door flew open, hitting her squarely in the face. She jerked back and fell to the floor, narrowly missing the edge of the bed. Her vision blurred, and something warm and wet streamed from her nose. She pressed her throbbing forehead and felt a knot beginning to form In the darkness, a shadow of a figure came closer and closer, but she couldn't make out who it was. The hairs on the nape of her neck lifted. Then he bent over her, and she let out a small cry. It was Federico. He pulled her up with one hand and pushed her roughly back on the bed. In his other hand, he was carrying a rifle.

She blinked rapidly and jammed her hands into her armpits, trying to protect herself. Her mouth moved, but she couldn't speak.

"You shut up and listen," he said. "Now you're going to go to the police and tell them it was all a lie about me. I didn't do anything to you, and you just made it up."

Maria nodded. "Okay." She was shivering from head to toe.

He smirked. "Not until after I have my fun. You're single now, after all. Forget about Salvatore. You're mine now."

Maria was nauseated. She couldn't go through this again. She wouldn't. It would destroy her completely, but she had no energy to fight this horrible man. Yet, what choice did she have? She couldn't let herself die because she had to protect her children from this man.

A pain shot through her chest. She could hardly breathe, but she had to do something. Otherwise she'd have to give herself to this man.

Footsteps sounded in the hallway. Then Roberto burst into the room, punching and shouting at Federico. Unbalanced, Federico dropped the rifle. Roberto made a dash for it, but Federico was too quick. He scooped up the rifle and pointed it at Roberto, who stared into his eyes, breathing hard but unflinching. Maria had never been prouder of her son, but she was also terrified.

Images flashed through her mind, visions of her son lying crumpled on the floor, a pool of blood spreading around him. No, it couldn't happen. She wouldn't let it. Maria launched herself off the bed. "No, please take me. Leave my son out of this. I'm all yours." She turned to Roberto. "Please go. I'll be alright."

Roberto's eyes were grim. "No, Mama. He won't hurt you again. I'm here to protect you."

Federico laughed. "You? You couldn't kill a cockroach. You're a kid."

Roberto glanced around as if trying to come up with a plan. Before Federico could lift the rifle, Maria snatched the bedside lamp nearby and swung it as hard as she could. It caught Federico on the side of the head, knocking him sideways. He bounced off the wall and fell to the ground, moaning.

Roberto reached across the fallen man and grabbed her hand. "Let's get out of here. Mama. Now!"

She dropped the lamp and jumped over Federico's legs as he struggled to get up. He snatched at her foot, and she kicked him in the head and ran.

They were almost out the door when Angela and Edoardo bumped into them. Andrea sat behind them, frozen in his wheelchair.

Maria suddenly felt Federico's rough hand grab her hard by the shoulder. She tried to free herself, but he jerked back and held her tightly across the waist with her arms trapped underneath his. He pointed the rifle at her children.

"No!" She shook her head, blinded by terror. The sound of his voice chilled her to the core.

"You're not going anywhere. Now get to the living room or I'll shoot the lot of you."

For a moment, they wavered, questioning her with frightened eyes. He gestured with the rifle, and at her quick nod, the children turned and started down the hall. While Angela walked ahead, Roberto whispered something to Edoardo, who gave a quick nod. Then before Federico could stop him, Edoardo bolted into the boy's room, jumped over the bed, shoved open the window and tumbled out.

Federico quickly closed the door and trapped them in the room, pointing the rifle at them. "Anyone moves and they're dead." Quickly, he moved over to the window, and, glancing from the window to the hostages, pointed the rifle at Edoardo. His finger tightened on the trigger.

Maria stopped breathing. She ran for her life towards him and shoved the barrel of the rifle away from her son. The crack of the rifle rang in her ears, and a spray of bark and sawdust flew up from a nearby tree.

Edoardo ran for his life.

The breath Maria had been holding burst out of her. "Run, Edoardo, run. She was proud of his courage. With narrow eyes, Federico whirled and smashed the butt of the gun across her head. She fell, ears ringing across Edoardo's bed.

"Mama, no!" Angela cried. Both Angela and Roberto headed to their mother, stroking her bleeding face. Andrea reached for tissues but Federico stopped him with a hard stare. You know what?" Federico said with an ugly smirk. "If he's gone to find Salvatore, then let him. He won't like what he finds when he gets here."

Maria felt chills all over her body. Angela's scream was cut short by Federico's cold glare. Then Roberto said, "You don't know how fast Edoardo is. You'd better get out of here while you still can."

With an ugly laugh, Federico pushed them all towards the living room, the rifle pointing at them as he followed them into the hall.

Chapter 38

DEATH

Federico roamed the living room with the rifle in his hand. He squinted, looking flushed and on edge. The children were trembling. They sat on the couch and kept their eyes focused on the ground.

Maria looked up at their captor. "What do you really want? Just tell me and leave the children alone."

He headed towards her, inches from her face as he bowed down to her level. "You ain't in a position to tell me what to do, so just shut up." He turned towards Roberto. "Now, I want you to tie up Angela." The veins in Federico's forehead stuck out as he grabbed some rope from his back pockets. He handed it to Roberto to tie up his sister. "Anyone try to get the rifle and I'll stab them. I have a switchblade with me too."

"Please, enough with the threats. We'll do as you ask," Maria said.

"I want you to get Andrea out of that wheelchair and put him on the floor over there." He pointed to the doorway leading to the kitchen. Maria shuddered, wondering what he was planning. Without argument, she headed to Andrea, lifted him out of his wheelchair, carried him through the doorway and laid him gently on the kitchen floor. Her back twinged as she straightened, but she forced herself not to wince.

Federico ordered Roberto to tie Andrea's hands to the kitchen table with spare rope in his other pocket. He then tied up Roberto to the leg of the couch. Maria sat back on the couch, waiting and watching with a sinking feeling in her stomach. Would Edoardo make it back in time? What was their fate? She thought again of Isabella's warning and pressed her palms hard against her stomach.

Federico stormed over to the kitchen and opened up the fridge. Keeping the rifle at his side, he made himself a sandwich and devoured it as if he'd never eaten in his life. He ate with his mouth open and licked his fingers. Then he cleaned his mouth on the tea towel and threw it on the ground.

Maria's lip curled. She'd definitely have to throw out that tea towel.

"Listen," she said, fidgeting as she spoke. "Why don't we go to the police station now? I—I can tell them exactly what you want, then you can leave us alone. You can go wherever you like and they won't have any reason to search for you."

Federico headed towards her. "Shut up, I'm thinking." He paced the floor in deep thought. "This is how it's going to play out. I'm going to shoot all of your children, then, Maria, you'll be coming with me." He licked his lips. "I guess we can forget about going to the police now. There's no point when I can have you all to myself without these loser kids getting in our way."

Maria felt like a statue. She saw the fear in her children's eyes, yet Roberto stood up to him. "No, let me go with you. Leave my Mama out of this."

Federico chuckled, then picked his teeth with a dirty fingernail. "And what would I do with you?" He pointed the rifle at Roberto, then turned to Maria. "You are beautiful, you know that? I sure am jealous of Salvatore." Maria turned away, avoiding his penetrating gaze. "Now you and me are going to make some beautiful music together."

Maria shook her head. "No please, I gave you my word. I'll let the police know you never hurt me. Just go as far away as you can."

"I will go far away, but you're coming with me." He grabbed her harshly by the shoulders while Angela yelled, "Mama, Mama. Please don't take her. Please!"

"Mama," Roberto said. "We'll be okay. Trust me."

From his place on the floor, Andrea sobbed. "I'm sorry, Maria. Sorry for what my Papa did to you. You didn't deserve that."

Roberto shook. "Wait! Are you really going to shoot us all? What about the police then? They'll definitely come looking for you. Salvatore will too, and he'll kill you."

"Oh, shut up." Federico sneered and pointed the rifle at Andrea. "I think I know just how to hurt Salvatore the most.

Maria grabbed him by the arm. "No, please, he's innocent. They're all innocent. Kill me, not them." She heard something rustling outside. Was it footsteps in the distance? Was something rustling in the bushes? She had to stall him until they came. "Where do you plan to go?"

"To our special place, darling. Where I plan to be entertained by you all night long. It's a place that nobody knows about, so no-one will find us there." He laughed, a chilly sound in the silent room, then walked over with heavy steps to where Andrea was trembling and crying. There was a wet patch on his pants, and Maria felt sick. This couldn't happen. She had to stop this man.

"So sorry, Andrea, it's nothing personal towards you. I just hate your dad." Before he could aim, Maria shoved him and wrestled him for the rifle. She heard the door slam open, and was suddenly shoved aside. Her heart leaped when she saw it was Salvatore. He jumped on Federico and pinned him to the ground, punching him a few times in the face. Federico bucked Salvatore off and rolled to his feet, then grabbed the rifle and pointed it at Salvatore.

"No!" Maria leaped at Federico, tugging at the rifle. Salvatore pushed Maria away and struggled with Federico for the rifle. He was pushing her away from danger, she realised. Risking his life for hers.

Maria glanced around the kitchen for a weapon. She snatched up a pot lying on the table and threw it at Federico. It landed on his foot, and he yelped with pain. Salvatore grabbed the rifle and pointed it at Federico.

From the living room, Roberto shouted, "The police are here."

Salvatore gestured with the rifle. "Jail for life, I believe." He glanced at Maria. "Are you okay?"

She nodded.

"And you, Andrea?" A flash of movement from Federico caught Maria's eye. Before she could shout a warning, he slipped the knife from his back pocket and plunged it into Salvatore's abdomen.

Maria cried out, watching in horror as Salvatore bent over in pain. As Federico bolted for the door, Salvatore raised the rifle and fired at him twice. Federico crumpled to the floor. Dead silence. Salvatore dropped the rifle and sank slowly to the ground, his shirt slick and red with blood. Maria knelt down and felt his wound. It was deep, and he was losing so much blood. "Don't you dare die on me, Salvatore. Don't you dare!" She grabbed a tea towel from the kitchen and pressed hard on the wound. "Press on this. I'll go get help."

He nodded. "Car—near—near house." His eyes fluttered shut, and his head lolled to one side. Beneath her hand, the tea towel was already soaked.

"Salvatore, stay awake. Please. Damn it, stay awake."

Andrea's body went still and Roberto said, "Untie us and we'll help."

She didn't want to leave Salvatore's side, but she had no choice. Quickly, she found a knife and cut Roberto's ropes. As she worked, Edoardo came in, breathless, and helped untie the others. Together, they lifted Salvatore and carried him to the car.

Giovanni's sweet face, pale and sweating, flashed through her mind. This could not be happening again.

Maria settled Salvatore in the back seat and turned to Roberto.

"You need to watch the kids. I'll be back as soon as I know anything." He nodded, a dark expression on his face. "And please, take care of Andrea. He's in shock."

As her sons walked back inside, she jumped into the car. The keys were still in the ignition. Thank God for that. She turned on the motor with her foot on the accelerator. The car shot forward, narrowly missing a tree. Salvatore moaned.

"Hang on," she muttered. "Just hang on."

Veering straight ahead, she aimed the car down the road towards Salerno. She had to get Salvatore to the hospital before he bled out.

Chapter 39

MOVING FORWARD

A week later, Roberto, his mother, and siblings sat in the Salerno Hospital on hard-backed chairs. Andrea, looking pale and teary-eyed stretched upward in his wheelchair and peered out the window of his father's hospital room. He glanced towards Salvatore, concern in his eyes.

Maria's hands were clasped tightly in her lap as she asked, "So did the police come and get your statement?"

"They did," Salvatore said. "Case closed as Federico's dead." His eyes darkened. "I'm sorry, Maria for all the wrong that I've done. I should've died that night but I guess God had other plans for me."

Andrea turned away from the window. "You be quiet, Papa. I never ever wanted you dead. You saved us from that monster. I now know who the real monster was."

"I'm sorry son. For not being a better father or husband to your mother. I promise that things will change from now on."

Roberto watched as his mother turned away and joined Andrea. She embraced him and stroked his hair. Angela and Edoardo joined her, huddled around Andrea. Was there hope for Mama and Salvatore? It did seem as if Salvatore was a different man; a changed man, and maybe they needed to give him another chance. His mother turned back to Salvatore.

Salvatore's eyes suddenly squeezed shut, and he let out a quiet moan.

Mama hurried to the bed and touched his shoulder. "What's wrong?"

"Oh, the pain is unbearable. Just tell me something to take my mind off the pain. Please, anything."

"Well, I'll fix us a nice dinner next week because Filippo's coming home, and I expect you to come. He's doing well in his job and just got a pay increase. He saved up enough to come by for a few weeks. Isn't that great?"

"I can't wait to see him, Mama," said Angela.

Edoardo made a face. "Oh, now there'll be less room at home."

"I really miss him," Roberto said. I guess he has a lot to catch up on."

Roberto held a bag in his hand and felt the weight of it. He felt it was the right time to give this gift to his Mama, and had worked on it until late the night before. He headed to his mother, took out the olive-wood box and handed it to her.

Maria furrowed her brow. "What's this?"

"Papa made most of this box before he died. I finally finished it for you last night." Roberto watched Salvatore as Maria opened it, feeling the smoothness of the wood inside the box. Salvatore looked hurt at first, then said, "I realise now that Giovanni was a decent and honourable man. I know he'll always have a place in your hearts, and I'm fine with that. I appreciate it too."

Maria beamed, shedding tears. "This is absolutely beautiful," she said to Roberto. "Thank you, darling." She moved towards Roberto and held him tightly.

After a few moments of awkward silence, Salvatore knit his brows and tried to lift himself up in the bed. Mama helped him. "Thanks. Hey listen, children. Can I have a few minutes alone with your mother?"

The children walked out of the ward, but Roberto stayed near the edge of the walkway, listening in. Their voices were clear and he hoped they couldn't see him.

"I want a second chance, Maria. A chance to prove myself to you." He waited, but Mama said nothing. "I'm a changed man, and I know that I have to communicate more. That way, I'll be less likely to resort to manipulation. I love you so much. I never stopped loving you, my dearest Maria."

"I love you too, Salvatore, but—"

"But what?"

"You have to earn back my trust. Don't think we're back together. You can stay in the house, but we'll have separate bedrooms until I can learn to trust you again. It could take months or even years. I can't promise you anything right now."

"That's all I ask, Maria. A chance to prove myself. I promise—you'll realise how much I've changed. I've been miserable without you and the kids. Your kids—I love them like my own."

Roberto was interrupted by the sound of a yell from Andrea behind him. It was a happy yell. He turned towards Andrea and the others.

"What is it?"

Andrea pointed towards his feet. His toes were slowly moving. "I can feel my legs and feet. I can even move them. That has to be a good sign, doesn't it?"

Roberto beamed. They all entered the ward and gave Salvatore and his mother the great news. Salvatore's face brightened as if all the weight of the last months lifted off his shoulders. Maria headed towards Andrea and hugged him tightly.

"That's amazing news, darling" she said. "You'll be walking pretty soon. I'll call the doctor."

His mother left the room and Roberto breathed easily for the first time in a long time. Finally, he knew that all was well in his world.

Reviews are gold to authors and allow Lucy to keep writing. If you enjoyed the story, please consider rating and reviewing it here: https://books2read.com/u/bpqwk3

Check out the future of Roberto's life with Valeria (The Italian Family Series) in *A New Life (FREE Novella)*: https://books2read.com/u/mqqwZm

<u>Read more books in the Italian Family Series:</u>

Dancing In The Rain:

https://books2read.com/u/bOr7LA

A Life By Design:

https://books2read.com/u/3J8ene

ABOUT THE AUTHOR

Lucy Appadoo is a prolific reader and author of the Friends In Crisis and Women Of Strength Series. After a childhood spent reading and imagining escapist worlds, Lucy has put her imagination into stories. Her work as a rehabilitation counsellor, and former work as a counsellor in private practice, have led to an interest in writing inspirational stories about authentic, driven women who manage adversity with strength and heart. She writes in the genres of romantic suspense/thrillers with significant life themes and contemporary romance.

Lucy's interests include researching crime stories and news to inspire her work, watching crime thrillers and suspenseful movies, travel, exercising, reading for entertainment or knowledge, meditation, and spending time with friends and family. She also appreciates her

Italian background and culture, which has inspired her to write imaginative stories about her parents' childhoods, leading to The Italian Family Series novels.

Check out Lucy's website and sign up for a FREE book: https://www.lucyappadooauthor.com.au

ALSO BY LUCY APPADOO

Web Of Lies (Book 3):

https://books2read.com/u/3JXazE

Love-Obsessed (Book 4):

https://books2read.com/u/4jPKGX

The Hearts Series - Romantic Suspense

Rising Hearts (Book 1):

https://books2read.com/u/mZwpoE

Forbidden Hearts (Book 2):

https://books2read.com/u/bQBKr7

Kindred Hearts (Book 3):

https://books2read.com/u/4AJKQK

Broken Hearts (prequel to Forbidden Hearts):

https://books2read.com/u/mgrnOD

Short Story Thrillers

Evening Interrupted:

https://books2read.com/u/3yZDjZ

The Dreamcatcher: https://books2read.com/u/bzaLxn

Red Flags: https://books2read.com/u/bWZ9W1

Collection of Short Story Thrillers:

https://books2read.com/u/bP5vwj

The Italian Family Series - Coming of Age Family Drama/Romance

A New Life: https://books2read.com/u/mqqwZm

Dancing in the Rain: https://books2read.com/u/bOr7LA

A Life By Design: https://books2read.com/u/3J8ene

NON-FICTION

Grief & Loss

Moving Beyond Grief - How To Shift From Grief & Loss to Joy & Peace: https://books2read.com/u/mVNzDA

Stress Management & Anxiety

Holistic Spiritual and Mental Health - Building Resilience and Creativity by Conquering Anxiety and Managing Stress: https://books2read.com/u/47kG8A

Career Guidance

Your Holistic Career Path - Create Career Change, Satisfaction, and Work/Life Balance: https://books2read.com/u/bzYDz4

www.ingramcontent.com/pod-product-compliance
Lightning Source LLC
Chambersburg PA
CBHW020911130726
47904CB00006BA/1832